BURIED ALIVE

ARNOLD BENNETT

BURIED ALIVE

ALAN SUTTON

First published 1912

First published in this edition in the United Kingdom in 1991 by
Alan Sutton Publishing Limited · Phoenix Mill · Far Thrupp · Stroud
Gloucestershire

British Library Cataloguing in Publication Data

Bennett, Alan, *1867–1931*
　Buried alive.
　I. Title
　823.912 [F]

ISBN 0–7509–0008–3

Cover Picture: detail from An Artist in his Studio *by Pascale Adolphe Jean Dagnan
Bouveret (Photograph: Fine Art Photograpic Library Ltd)*

Typeset in 9/10 Bembo.
Typesetting and origination by
Alan Sutton Publishing Limited.
Printed in Great Britain by
The Guernsey Press Company Limited,
Guernsey, Channel Islands.

CONTENTS

BIOGRAPHICAL NOTE

ARNOLD BENNETT (1867–1931) was a successful, prolific and versatile writer, now best known as a novelist whose major works introduced the mainstream of European realism to early twentieth-century English Literature. He presented the seamy side of provincial life, dispassionately recording its ugly and sordid features, sometimes ironically and always without censure, in a series of over thirty novels and collections of short stories. Yet he was the author of more than seventy books in all, a cosmopolitan and industrious journalist who performed at many levels of seriousness, a perceptive critic of contemporary music, literature and art, as well as a playwright and essayist who became a popular figure in the early twentieth-century literary establishment.

(Enoch) Arnold Bennett was born on 27 May 1867 at Hanley, Staffordshire, one of the 'Five Towns' (properly six) of the Potteries now comprising Stoke-on-Trent. The eldest of six children of a self-made Methodist provincial solicitor (who had also been a schoolmaster), he was brought up in an atmosphere of sturdy middle-class respectability and self-improvement of an uncommonly cultured and bookish household. He was educated at the Burslem Endowed School and the Middle School at Newcastle-under-Lyme, later attending a local art school (he painted charming watercolours to the end of his life). At the age of eighteen he worked as a clerk in his father's office, where he contributed precocious weekly articles to a local newspaper.

He left the Potteries in 1889 for London where, after a period articled to a firm of solicitors, he soon put aside his law studies and laboured to establish himself in journalism. He wrote popular and sensational serial fiction, becoming assistant editor (1894), and later editor (1896–1900), of a women's magazine, *Woman*, where he wrote on a variety of topics from society gossip, fashion and recipes to book and, above all, theatre reviews. His writing was increasingly in demand from other magazines, including the leading critical journal *Academy*, and the popular press. Encouraged by the publication of a short story in the fashionable *Yellow Book* in July 1895, he embarked on a first novel, which was published in 1898 as *A Man from the North*.

In 1900 he resigned his editorship of *Woman* to become a professional writer, continuing to contribute free-lance short stories and serial novels to magazines. *The Grand Babylon Hotel* (1902), a sensational and popular work in the manner of Ouida, was published in the same year as *Anna of the Five Towns* (1902), a work of serious literary pretensions under the influence of George Moor and Émile Zola. This is now considered one of his best novels, describing against the fictional background of the Five Towns of the Staffordshire Potteries a heroine of honesty and compassion who refuses to compromise with provincial Methodist society.

In 1903, after his father's death, he moved from a farmhouse in the Bedfordshire countryside to metropolitan Paris, in the footsteps of the artists and writers whom he most admired. In Paris he conceived his greatest and best known novel, *The Old Wives' Tale* (1908), which established, and has since largely maintained, his reputation. This is a novel of finely drawn characters set against a vividly realized background: the heroines are two sisters, one allegedly inspired by an ungainly elderly woman whom he had seen in a Paris restaurant in 1903. When the *Clayhanger* trilogy appeared (1910–1916; reprinted 1925 as *The Clayhanger Family*), his stature as one of the leading serious novelists of the day was confirmed. Showing him as a meticulous and often comic dramatist and historian of life in the Five Towns, it concerns the gloomy life of Edwin Clayhanger and his desperate love for Hilda Lessways and, in the final volume, their life together.

In Paris, Bennett wrested free of his provincial attitudes, becoming a cosmopolitan inhabitant of the Paris of the end of the *belle époque*, a melting-pot of artistic and literary ifluences and experiment. An early admirer of the French masters, who had been among the first English novelists to learn from studying the technique of Balzac, Flaubert, the de Goncourts, de Maupassant and Zola, his criticism is of a high order; it demonstrates his early appreciation of the contemporary arts, of the Post-impressionist painters, of the ballet of Diaghilev and Stravinsky, as well as of the young writers, including Joyce, D.H. Lawrence and Faulkner. In 1907 he married a French actress, Marguerite Soulié, from whom he was separated in 1921.

When, after ten years in Paris, Bennett returned to England, he was a figure of the literary establishment, rich beyond the dreams of most authors, and offered a knighthood (in 1918; which he declined). He divided his time between London, Paris, a yacht and a country house in Essex, never returning to the Potteries except for brief visits, although they were to continue to provide the imaginative background to his novels. He wrote with remarkable facility, publishing novels and short stories, working as a journalist (particularly a powerful propagandist during the War years, and before them in A. R. Orage's brilliant journal, *New Age*) and writing a number of plays. The latter include *Milestones* (1912; with E. Knoblock) and *The Great Adventure* (1913; adapted from an earlier novel), which were popular successes.

A precursor of modernism who owed much to the example of the European realists, his reputation suffered a decline after the great novels of the pre-war years: the modernists condemned his technique as providing mere 'photography', for its excessively scientific and unstructured accumulation of details. From this it was retrieved by the publication in 1923 of *Riceyman Steps*, the last of his major novels and a popular and critical success. It is a brilliant achievement in technique and design, set in the dark and squalid suburbs of London. . . The sinister tale concerns a miserly second-hand-book dealer who starves himself to death and whose contagious passion for thrift dominates his household, with terrible consequences for his wife. Here Bennett's handling of atmosphere, his psychological observation and kindly tolerance of feeling contribute to a final masterpiece.

In 1924 Arnold Bennett was moved to complete the novella *Elsie and the Child – A Tale of Riceyman Steps* reintroducing Elsie from the original novel, now working with her husband Joe in the household of Dr Raste.

The Journals of Arnold Bennett 1896–1928, a fascinating account of his life and times, were edited by Newman Flower (3 vols., 1932–3) after his death of typhoid fever in Marylebone, London, on 27 March 1931.

NICHOLAS MANDER

CHAPTER I

THE PUCE DRESSING-GOWN

The peculiar angle of the earth's axis to the plan of the ecliptic – that angle which is chiefly responsible for our geography and therefore our history – had caused the phenomenon known in London as summer. The whizzing globe happened to have turned its most civilized face away from the sun, thus producing night in Selwood Terrace, South Kensington. In No. 91 Selwood Terrace two lights, on the ground-floor and on the first-floor, were silently proving that man's ingenuity can outwit Nature. No. 91 was one of about ten thousand similar houses between South Kensington Station and North End Road. With its grimy stucco front, its cellar kitchen, its hundred stairs and steps, its perfect inconvenience, and its conscience heavy with the doing to death of sundry general servants, it uplifted tin chimney-cowls to heaven and gloomily awaited the day of judgment for London houses, sublimely ignoring the axial and orbital velocities of the earth and even the reckless flight of the whole solar system through space. You felt that No. 91 was unhappy, and that it could only be rendered happy by a 'To let' standard in its front patch and a 'No bottles' card in its windows. It possessed neither of these specifics. Though of late generally empty, it was never untenanted. In the entire course of its genteel and commodious career, it had never once been to let.

Go inside, and breathe its atmosphere of a bored house that is generally empty yet never untenanted. All its twelve rooms dark and forlorn, save two; its cellar kitchen dark and forlorn; just these two rooms, one on the top of the other like boxes, pitifully struggling against the inveterate gloom of the remaining ten! Stand in the dark hall and get this atmosphere into your lungs.

The principal, the startling thing in the illuminated room on the ground-floor was a dressing-gown, of the colour, between

1

heliotrope and purple, known to a previous generation as puce; a quilted garment stuffed with swansdown, light as hydrogen – nearly, and warm as the smile of a kind heart; old, perhaps, possibly worn in its outlying regions and allowing fluffs of feathery white to escape through its satin pores; but a dressing-gown to dream of. It dominated the unkempt, naked apartment, its voluptuous folds glittering crudely under the sun-replacing oil lamp which was set on a cigar box on the stained deal table. The oil lamp had a glass reservoir, a chipped chimney, and a cardboard shade, and had probably cost less than a florin; five florins would have purchased the table; and all the rest of the furniture, including the arm-chair in which the dressing-gown reclined, a stool, an easel, three packets of cigarettes, and a trouser-stretcher, might have been replaced for another ten florins. Up in the corners of the ceiling, obscure in the eclipse of the cardboard shade, was a complicated system of cobwebs to match the dust on the bare floor.

Within the dressing-gown there was a man. This man had reached the interesting age. I mean the age when you think you have shed all the illusions of infancy, when you think you understand life, and when you are often occupied in speculating upon the delicious surprises which existence may hold for you; the age, in sum, that is the most romantic and tender of all ages – for a male. I mean the age of fifty. An age absurdly misunderstood by all those who have not reached it! A thrilling age! Appearances are tragically deceptive.

The inhabitant of the puce dressing-gown had a short greying beard and moustache; his plenteous hair was passing from pepper into salt; there were many minute wrinkles in the hollows between his eyes and the fresh crimson of his cheeks; and the eyes were sad; they were very sad. Had he stood erect and looked perpendicularly down, he would have perceived not his slippers, but a protuberant button of the dressing-gown. Understand me: I conceal nothing; I admit the figures written in the measurement-book of his tailor. He was fifty. Yet, like most men of fifty, he was still very young, and, like most bachelors of fifty, he was rather helpless. He was quite sure that he had not had the best of luck. If he had excavated his soul he would have discovered somewhere in its deeps a wistful, appealing desire to be taken care of, to be sheltered from the inconveniences and harshness of the world. But he would not have admitted the discovery. A bachelor of fifty cannot be expected to admit even that he resembles a girl of nineteen. Nevertheless it is a strange fact that the resemblance between the heart of an experienced, adventurous bachelor of fifty and the simple heart of a girl of nineteen is stronger than girls of nineteen imagine; especially when the bachelor of fifty is sitting solitary and unfriended at two o'clock in the night, in the forlorn atmosphere of a house that has outlived its hopes. Bachelors of fifty alone will comprehend me.

It has never been decided what young girls do meditate upon when they meditate; young girls themselves cannot decide. As a rule the lonely fancies of middle-aged bachelors are scarcely less amenable to definition. But the case of the inhabitant of the puce dressing-gown was an exception to the rule. He knew, and he could have said, precisely what he was thinking about. In that sad hour and place, his melancholy thoughts were centred upon the resplendent, unique success in life of a gifted and glorious being known to nations and newspapers as Priam Farll.

RICHES AND RENOWN

In the days when the New Gallery was new, a picture, signed by the unknown name of Priam Farll, was exhibited there, and aroused such terrific interest that for several months no conversation among cultured persons was regarded as complete without some reference to it. That the artist was a very great painter indeed was admitted by every one; the only question which cultured persons felt it their duty to settle was whether he was the greatest painter that ever lived, or merely the greatest painter since Velasquez. Cultured persons might have continued to discuss that nice point to the present hour, had it not leaked out that the picture had been refused by the Royal Academy. The culture of London then at once healed up its strife and combined to fall on the Royal Academy as an institution which had no right to exist. The affair even got into Parliament, and occupied three minutes of the imperial legislature. Useless for the Royal Academy to argue that it had overlooked the canvas, for its dimensions were seven feet by five; it represented a policeman, a simple policeman, life-size, and it was not merely the most striking portrait imaginable, but the first appearance of the policeman in great art; criminals, one heard, instinctively fled before it. No! The Royal Academy really could not argue that the work had been overlooked. And in truth the Royal Academy did not argue accidental negligence. It did not argue about its own right to exist. It did not argue at all. It blandly went on existing, and taking about a hundred and fifty pounds a day in shillings at its polished turn-stiles. No details were obtainable concerning Priam Farll, whose address was Poste Restante, St Martin's-le-Grand. Various collectors, animated by deep faith in their own judgment and a sincere desire to encourage British art, were anxious to purchase the picture for a few pounds, and these enthusiasts were astonished and pained to learn that Priam Farll had marked a figure of £1,000 – the price of a rare postage stamp.

In consequence the picture was not sold; and after an enterprising journal had unsuccessfully offered a reward for the identification of the portrayed policeman, the matter went gently to sleep while the pubic employed its annual holiday as usual in discussing the big gooseberry of matrimonial relations.

Every one naturally expected that in the following year the mysterious Priam Farll would, in accordance with the universal rule for a successful career in British art, contribute another portrait of another policeman to the New Gallery – and so on for about twenty years, at the end of which period England would have learnt to recognize him as its favourite painter of policemen. But Priam Farll contributed nothing to the New Gallery. He had apparently forgotten the New Gallery: which was considered to be ungracious, if not ungrateful, on his part. Instead, he adorned the Paris salon with a large seascape showing penguins in the foreground. Now these penguins became the penguins of the continental year; they made penguins the fashionable bird in Paris, and also (twelve months later) in London. The French Government offered to buy the picture on behalf of the Republic at its customary price of five hundred francs, but Priam Farll sold it to the American connoisseur, Whitney C. Witt, for five thousand dollars. Shortly afterwards he sold the policeman, whom he had kept by him, to the same connoisseur for ten thousand dollars. Whitney C. Witt was the expert who had paid two hundred thousand dollars for a Madonna and St Joseph, with donor, of Raphael. The enterprising journal before mentioned calculated that, counting the space actually occupied on the canvas by the policeman, the daring connoisseur had expended two guineas per square inch on the policeman.

At which stage the vast newspaper public suddenly woke up and demanded with one voice –

'Who is this Priam Farll?'

Though the query remained unanswered, Priam Farll's reputation was henceforward absolutely assured, and this in spite of the fact that he omitted to comply with the regulations ordained by English society for the conduct of successful painters. He ought, first, to have taken the elementary precaution of being born in the United States. He ought, after having refused all interviews for months, to have ultimately granted a special one to a newspaper with the largest circulation. He ought to have returned to England, grown a mane and a tufted tail, and become the king of beasts; or at least to have made a speech at a banquet about the noble and purifying mission of art. Assuredly he ought to have painted the portrait of his father or grandfather as an artisan, to prove that he was not a snob. But no! Not content with making each of his pictures utterly different from all the others, he neglected all the above formalities – and yet managed to pile triumph on triumph. There are some men of whom it may be said that, like a punter on a good day, they can't do wrong. Priam Farll was one such. In a few years he had become a legend, a standing side-dish of a riddle. No one knew him; no one saw him; no one married him. Constantly abroad, he was ever the subject of conflicting rumours. Parfitts themselves, his London agents, knew naught of him but his handwriting – on the backs of cheques in four figures. They sold an average of five large and five small pictures for him every year. These pictures arrived out of the unknown and the cheques went into the unknown.

Young artists, mute in admiration before the master-pieces from his brush which enriched all the national galleries of

Europe (save, of course, that in Trafalgar Square), dreamt of
him, worshipped him, and quarrelled fiercely about him, as
the very symbol of glory, luxury and flawless accomplishment, never conceiving him as a man like themselves, with
boots to lace up, a palette to clean, a beating heart, and an
instinctive fear of solitude.

Finally there came to him the paramount distinction, the last
proof that he was appreciated. The press actually fell into the
habit of mentioning his name without explanatory comment.
Exactly as it does not write 'Mr A.J. Balfour, the eminent
statesman,' or 'Sarah Bernhardt, the renowned actress,' or
'Charles Peace, the historic murderer,' but simply 'Mr A.J.
Balfour,' 'Sarah Bernhardt,' or 'Charles Peace'; so it wrote
simply 'Mr Priam Farll.' And no occupant of a smoker in a
morning train ever took his pipe out of his mouth to ask,
'What is the johnny?' Greater honour in England hath no man.
Priam Farll was the first English painter to enjoy this supreme
social reward.

And now he was inhabiting the puce dressing-gown.

THE DREADFUL SECRET

A bell startled the forlorn house; its loud old-fashioned jangle
came echoingly up the basement stairs and struck the ear of
Priam Farll, who half rose and then sat down again. He knew
that it was an urgent summons to the front door, and that
none but he could answer it; and yet he hesitated.

Leaving Priam Farll, the great and wealthy artist, we return
to that far more interesting person, Priam Farll the private
human creature; and come at once to the dreadful secret of his
character, the trait in him which explained the peculiar
circumstances of his life.

As a private human creature, he happened to be shy.

He was quite different from you or me. We never feel secret
qualms at the prospect of meeting strangers, or of taking
quarters at a grand hotel, or of entering a large house for the
first time, or of walking across a room full of seated people, or
of dismissing a servant, or of arguing with a haughty female
aristocrat behind a post-office counter, or of passing a shop

where we owe money. And for blushing or hanging back, or even looking awkward when faced with any such simple, everyday acts, the idea of conduct so childish would not occur to us. We behave naturally under all circumstances – for why should a sane man behave otherwise? Priam Farll was different. To call the world's attention visually to the fact of his own existence was anguish to him. But in a letter he could be absolutely brazen. Give him a pen and he was fearless.

Now he knew that he would have to go and open the front door. Both humanity and self-interest urged him to go instantly. For the visitant was assuredly the doctor come at last to see the sick man lying upstairs. The sick man was Henry Leek, and Henry Leek was Priam Farll's bad habit. While somewhat of a rascal (as his master guessed), Leek was a very perfect valet. Like you and me, he was never shy. He always did the natural thing naturally. He had become, little by little, indispensable to Priam Farll, the sole means of living communication between Priam Farll and the universe of men. The master's shyness, resembling a deer's, kept the pair almost entirely out of England, and, on their continuous travels, the servant invariably stood between that sensitive diffidence and the world. Leek saw every one who had to be seen, and did everything that involved personal contacts. And, being a bad habit, he had of course grown on Priam Farll, and thus, year after year, for a quarter of a century, Farll's shyness, with his riches and his glory, had increased. Happily Leek was never ill. That is to say, he never had been ill, until this day of their sudden incognito arrival in London for a brief sojourn. He could hardly have chosen a more inconvenient moment; for in London of all places, in that inherited house in Selwood Terrace which he so seldom used, Priam Farll could not carry on daily life without him. It really was unpleasant and disturbing in the highest degree, this illness of Leek's. The fellow had apparently caught cold on the night-boat. He had fought the approaches of insidious disease for several hours, going forth to make purchases and incidentally consulting a doctor; and then, without warning, in the very act of making up Priam Farll's couch, he had abandoned the struggle, and, since his own bed was not ready, he had taken to his master's.

He always did the natural thing naturally. And Farll had been forced to help him to undress!

From this point onwards Priam Farll, opulent though he was and illustrious, had sunk to a tragic impotence. He could do nothing for himself; and he could do nothing for Leek, because Leek refused both brandy and sandwiches, and the larder consisted solely of brandy and sandwiches. The man lay upstairs there, comatose, still, silent, waiting for the doctor who had promised to pay an evening visit. And the summer day had darkened into the summer night.

The notion of issuing out into the world, and personally obtaining food for himself or aid for Leek, did genuinely seem to Priam Farll an impossible notion; he had never done such things. For him a shop was an impregnable fort garrisoned by ogres. Besides, it would have been necessary to 'ask,' and 'asking' was the torture of tortures. So he had wandered, solicitous and helpless, up and down the stairs, until at length Leek, ceasing to be a valet and deteriorating into a mere human organism, had feebly yet curtly requested to be just let alone, asserting that he was right enough. Whereupon the envied of all painters, the symbol of artistic glory and triumph, had assumed the valet's notorious puce dressing-gown and established himself in a hard chair for a night of discomfort.

The bell rang once more, and there was a sharp impressive knock that reverberated through the forlorn house in a most portentous and terrifying manner. It might have been Death knocking. It engendered the horrible suspicion, 'Suppose he's *seriously* ill?' Priam Farll sprang up nervously, braced to meet ringers and knockers.

CURE FOR SHYNESS

On the other side of the door, dressed in frock coat and silk hat, there stood hesitating a tall, thin, weary man who had been afoot for exactly twenty hours, in pursuit of his usual business of curing imaginary ailments by means of medicine and suggestion, and leaving real ailments to nature aided by coloured water. His attitude towards the medical profession

was somewhat sardonic, partly because he was convinced that
only the gluttony of South Kensington provided him with a
livelihood, but more because his wife and two fully developed
daughters spent too much on their frocks. For years, losing
sight of the fact that he was an immortal soul, they had been
treating him as a breakfast-in-the-slot machine: they put a
breakfast in the slot, pushed a button on his waistcoat, and
drew out bank-notes. For this, he had neither partner nor
assistant, nor carriage, nor holiday: his wife and daughters
could not afford him these luxuries. He was able, conscien-
tious, chronically tired, bald, and fifty. He was also, strange as
it may seem, shy; though indeed he had grown used to it, as a
man gets used to a hollow tooth or an eel to skinning. No
qualities of the young girl's heart about the heart of Dr
Cashmore! He really did know human nature, and he never
dreamt of anything more paradisaical than a Sunday Pullman
escapade to Brighton.

Priam Farll opened the door which divided these two
hesitating men, and they saw each other by the light of the gas
lamp (for the hall was in darkness).

'This Mr Farll's?' asked Dr Cashmore, with the uninten-
tional asperity of shyness.

As for Priam, the revelation of his name by Leek shocked
him almost into a sweat. Surely the number of the house
should have sufficed.

'Yes,' he admitted, half shy and half vexed. 'Are you the
doctor?'

'Yes.'

Dr Cashmore stepped into the obscurity of the hall.

'How's the invalid going on?'

'I can scarcely tell you,' said Priam. 'He's in bed, very quiet.'

'That's right,' said the doctor. 'When he came to my surgery
this morning I advised him to go to bed.'

Then followed a brief, awkward pause, during which Priam
Farll coughed and the doctor rubbed his hands and hummed a
fragment of melody.

'By Jove!' the thought flashed through the mind of Farll.
'This chap's shy, I do believe!'

And through the mind of the doctor, 'Here's another of 'em,
all nerves!'

They both instantly, from sheer good-natured condescension the one to the other, became at ease. It was as if a spring had been loosed. Priam shut the door and shut out the ray of the street lamp.

'I'm afraid there's no light here,' said Dr Cashmore.

'I'll strike a match,' said Priam.

The flare of a wax vesta illumined the splendours of the puce dressing-gown. But Dr Cashmore did not blench. He could flatter himself that in the matter of dressing-gowns he had nothing to learn.

'By the way, what's wrong with him, do you think?' Priam Farll inquired in his most boyish voice.

'Don't know. Chill. He had a loud cardiac murmur. Might be anything. That's why I said I'd call anyhow to-night. Couldn't come any sooner. Been on my feet since six o'clock this morning. You know what it is – G.P.'s day.'

He smiled grimly in his fatigue.

'It's very good of you to come,' said Priam Farll with warm, vivacious sympathy. He had an astonishing gift for imaginatively putting himself in the place of other people.

'Not at all!' the doctor muttered. He was quite touched. To hide the fact that he was touched he struck a second match. 'Shall we go upstairs?'

In the bedroom a candle was burning on a dusty and empty dressing-table. Dr Cashmore moved it to the vicinity of the bed, which was like an oasis of decent arrangement in the desert of comfortless chamber; then he stooped to examine the sick valet.

'He's shivering!' exclaimed the doctor softly.

Henry Leek's skin was indeed bluish, though, besides blankets, there was a considerable apparatus of rugs on the bed, and the night was warm. His ageing face (for he was the third man of fifty in that room) had an anxious look. But he made no movement, uttered no word, at sight of the doctor; just stared dully. His own difficult breathing alone seemed to interest him.

'Any women up?'

The doctor turned suddenly and fiercely on Priam Farll, who started.

'There's only ourselves in the house,' he replied.

A person less experienced than Dr Cashmore in the secret strangeness of genteel life in London might have been astonished by this information. But Dr Cashmore no more blenched now than he had blenched at the puce garment.

'Well, hurry up and get some hot water,' said he, in a tone dictatorial and savage. 'Quick now! And brandy! And more blankets! Now don't stand there, please! Here! I'll go with you to the kitchen. Show me!' He snatched up the candle, and the expression of his features said, 'I can see you're no good in a crisis.'

'It's all up with me, doctor,' came a faint whisper from the bed.

'So it is, my boy!' said the doctor under his breath as he tumbled downstairs in the wake of Priam Farll. 'Unless I get something hot into you!'

MASTER AND SERVANT

'Will there have to be an inquest?' Priam Farll asked at 6 a.m.

He had collapsed on the hard chair on the ground-floor. The indispensable Henry Leek was lost to him for ever. He could not imagine what would happen to his existence in the future. He could not conceive himself without Leek. And, still worse, the immediate prospect of unknown horrors of publicity in connexion with the death of Leek overwhelmed him.

'No!' said the doctor cheerfully. 'Oh no! I was present. Acute double pneumonia! Sometimes happens like that! I can give a certificate. But of course you will have to go to the registrar's and register the death.'

Even without an inquest, Priam saw that the affair would be unthinkably distressing. He felt that it would kill him, and he put his hand to his face.

'Where are Mr Farll's relatives to be found?' the doctor asked.

'Mr Farll's relatives?' Priam Farll repeated without comprehending.

Then he understood. Dr Cashmore thought that Henry Leek's name was Farll! And all the sensitive timidity in Priam Farll's character seized swiftly at the mad chance of escape from any kind of public appearance as Priam Farll. Why should he not let it be supposed that he, and not Henry Leek, had expired suddenly in Selwood Terrace at 5 a.m.? He would be free, utterly free!

'Yes,' said the doctor. 'They must be informed naturally.'

Priam's mind ran rapidly over the catalogue of his family. He could think of no one nearer than a certain Duncan Farll, a second cousin.

'I don't think he had any,' he replied in a voice that trembled with excitement at the capricious rashness of what he was doing. 'Perhaps there were distant cousins. But Mr Farll never talked of them.'

Which was true.

He could scarcely articulate the words 'Mr Farll.' But when they were out of his mouth he felt that the deed was somehow definitely done.

The doctor gazed at Priam's hands, the rough, coarsened hands of a painter who is always messing in oils and dust.

'Pardon me,' said the doctor. 'I presume you are his valet – or — '

'Yes,' said Priam Farll.

That set the seal.

'What was your master's full name?' the doctor demanded.

And Priam Farll shivered.

'Priam Farll,' said he weakly.

'Not *the* — ?' loudly exclaimed the doctor, whom the hazards of life in London had at last staggered.

Priam nodded.

'Well, well!' The doctor gave vent to his feelings. The truth was that this particular hazard of life in London pleased him, flattered him, made him feel important in the world, and caused him to forget his fatigue and his wrongs.

He saw that the puce dressing-gown contained a man who was at the end of his tether, and with that good nature of his which no hardships had been able to destroy, he offered to attend to the preliminary formalities. Then he went.

A MONTH'S WAGES

Priam Farll had no intention of falling asleep; his desire was to consider the position which he had so rashly created for himself; but he did fall asleep – and in the hard chair! He was awakened by a tremendous clatter as if the house was being bombarded and there were bricks falling about his ears. When he regained all his senses this bombardment resolved itself into nothing but a loud and continued assault on the front door. He rose, and saw a frowsy, dishevelled, puce-coloured figure in the dirty mirror over the fireplace. And then, with stiff limbs, he directed his sleepy feet towards the door.

Dr Cashmore was at the door, and still another man of fifty, a stern-set blue-chinned, stoutish person in deep and perfect mourning, including black gloves.

This person gazed coldly at Priam Farll.

'Ah!' ejaculated the mourner.

And he stepped in, followed by Dr Cashmore.

In achieving the inner mat the mourner perceived a white square on the floor. He picked it up and carefully examined it, and then handed it to Priam Farll.

'I suppose this is for you,' said he.

Priam, accepting the envelope, saw that it was addressed to 'Henry Leek, Esq., 91 Selwood Terrace, S.W.,' in a woman's hand.

'It *is* for you, isn't it?' pursued the mourner in an inflexible voice.

'Yes,' said Priam.

'I am Mr Duncan Farll, a solicitor, a cousin of your late employer,' the metallic voice continued, coming through a set of large white teeth. 'What arrangements have you made during the day?'

Priam stammered: 'None. I've been asleep.'

'You aren't very respectful,' said Duncan Farll.

So this was his second cousin, whom he had met, once only, as a boy! Never would he have recognized Duncan. Evidently it did not occur to Duncan to recognize him. People are apt to grow unrecognizable in the course of forty years.

Duncan Farll strode about the ground-floor of the house, and on the threshold of each room ejaculated 'Ah!' or 'Ha!' Then he and the doctor went upstairs. Priam remained inert, and excessively disturbed, in the hall.

At length Duncan Farll descended.

'Come in here, Leek,' said Duncan.

And Priam meekly stepped after him into the room where the hard chair was. Duncan Farll took the hard chair.

'What are your wages?'

Priam sought to remember how much he had paid Henry Leek.

'A hundred a year,' said he.

'Ah! A good wage. When were you last paid?'

Priam remembered that he had paid Leek two days ago.

'The day before yesterday,' said he.

'I must say again you are not very respectful,' Duncan observed, drawing forth his pocket-book. 'However, here is £8 7s., a month's wages in lieu of notice. Put your things together, and go. I shall have no further use for you. I will make no observations of any kind. But be good enough to *dress* – it is three o'clock – and leave the house at once. Let me see your box or boxes before you go.'

When an hour later, in the gloaming, Priam Farll stood on the wrong side of his own door, with Henry Leek's heavy kit-bag and Henry Leek's tin trunk flanking him on either hand, he saw that events in his career were moving with immense rapidity. He had wanted to be free, and free he was. Quite free! But it appeared to him very remarkable that so much could happen, in so short a time, as the result of a mere momentary impulsive prevarication.

CHAPTER II

A PAIL

Sticking out of the pocket of Leek's light overcoat was a folded copy of the 'Daily Telegraph.' Priam Farll was something of a dandy, and like all right-thinking dandies and all tailors, he objected to the suave line of a garment being spoilt by a free utilization of pockets. The overcoat itself, and the suit beneath, were quite good; for, though they were the property of the late Henry Leek, they perfectly fitted Priam Farll and had recently belonged to him, Leek having been accustomed to clothe himself entirely from his master's wardrobe. The dandy absently drew forth the 'Telegraph,' and the first thing that caught his eye was this: 'A beautiful private hotel of the highest class. Luxuriously furnished. Visitors' comfort studied. Finest position in London. Cuisine a speciality. Suitable for persons of superior rank. Bath-room. Electric light. Separate tables. No irritating extras. Single rooms from 2½ guineas, double from 4 guineas weekly. 250 Queen's Gate.' And below this he saw another piece of news: 'Not a boarding-house. A magnificent mansion. Forty bedrooms by Waring. Superb public saloons by Maple. Parisian chef. Separate tables. Four bath-rooms. Card-room, billiard-room, vast lounge. Young, cheerful, musical society. Bridge (small). Special sanitation. Finest position in London. No irritating extras. Single rooms from 2½ guineas, double from 4 guineas weekly. 'Phone 10,073 Western. Trefusis Mansion, W.'

At that moment a hansom cab came ambling down Selwood Terrace.

Impulsively he hailed it.

''Ere, guv'nor,' said the cabman, seeing with an expert eye that Priam Farll was unaccustomed to the manipulation of luggage. 'Give this 'ere Hacken-schmidt a copper to lend ye a hand. You're only a light weight.'

A small and emaciated boy, with the historic remains of a cigarette in his mouth, sprang like a monkey up the steps, and, not waiting to be asked, snatched the trunk from Priam's hands. Priam gave him one of Leek's sixpences for his feats of strength, and the boy spit generously on the coin, at the same time, by a strange skill, clinging to the cigarette with his lower lip. Then the driver lifted the reins with a noble gesture, and Priam had to be decisive and get into the cab.

'250 Queen's Gate,' said he.

As, keeping his head to one side to avoid the reins, he gave the direction across the roof of the cab to the attentive cocked ear of the cabman, he felt suddenly that he had regained his nationality, that he was utterly English, in an atmosphere utterly English. The hansom was like home after the wilderness.

He had chosen 250 Queen's Gate because it appeared the abode of tranquillity and discretion. He felt that he might sink into 250 Queen's Gate as into a feather bed. The other place intimidated him. It recalled the terrors of a continental hotel. In his wanderings he had suffered much from the young, cheerful, and musical society of bright hotels, and bridge (small) had no attraction for him.

As the cab tinkled through canyons of familiar stucco, he looked further at the 'Telegraph.' He was rather surprised to find more than a column of enticing palaces, each in the finest position in London; London, in fact, seemed to be one unique, glorious position. And it was so welcome, so receptive, so wishful to make a speciality of your comfort, your food, your bath, your sanitation! He remembered the old boarding-houses of the 'eighties. Now all was changed, for the better. The 'Telegraph' was full of the better, crammed and packed with tight columns of it. The better burst aspiringly from the tops of columns on the first page and outsoared the very title of the paper. He saw there, for instance, to the left of the title, a new, refined tea-house in Piccadilly Circus, owned and managed by gentlewomen, where you had real tea and real bread and butter and real cakes in a real drawing-room. It was astounding.

The cab stopped.

'Is this it?' he asked the driver.

'This is 250, sir.'

And it was. But it did not resemble even a private hotel. It exactly resembled a private house, narrow and tall and squeezed in between its sister and its brother. Priam Farll was puzzled, till the solution occurred to him. 'Of course,' he said to himself. 'This is the quietude, the discretion. I shall like this.' He jumped down.

'I'll keep you,' he threw to the cabman, in the proper phrase (which he was proud to recall from his youth), as though the cabman had been something which he had ordered on approval.

There were two bell-knobs. He pulled one, and waited for the portals to open on discreet vistas of luxurious furniture. No response! Then he pulled the other knob. Still no response! Just as he was consulting the 'Telegraph' to make sure of the number, the door silently swung back, and disclosed the figure of a middle-aged woman in black silk, who regarded him with a stern astonishment.

'Is this — ?' he began, nervous and abashed by her formidable stare.

'Were you wanting rooms?' she asked.

'Yes,' said he. 'I was. If I could just see —'

'Will you come in?' she said. And her morose face, under stringent commands from her brain, began an imitation of a smile which, as an imitation, was wonderful. It made you wonder how she had ever taught her face to do it.

Priam Farll found himself blushing on a Turkey carpet, and a sort of cathedral gloom around him. He was disconcerted, but the Turkey carpet assured him somewhat. As his eyes grew habituated to the light he saw that the cathedral was very narrow, and that instead of the choir was a staircase, also clothed in Turkey carpet. On the lowest step reposed an object whose nature he could not at first determine.

'Would it be for long?' the lips opposite him muttered cautiously.

His reply – the reply of an impulsive, shy nature – was to rush out of the palace. He had identified the object on the stairs. It was a slop-pail with a wrung cloth on its head.

He felt profoundly discouraged and pessimistic. All his energy had left him. London had become hard, hostile, cruel, impossible. He longed for Leek with a great longing.

TEA

An hour later, having, at the kind suggestion of the cabman, deposited Leek's goods at the cloak-room of South Kensington Station, he was wandering on foot out of old London into the central ring of new London, where people never do anything except take the air in parks, lounge in club windows, roll to and fro in peculiar vehicles that have ventured out without horses and making the best of it, buy flowers and Egyptian cigarettes, look at pictures, and eat and drink. Nearly all the buildings were higher than they used to be, and the streets wider; and at intervals of a hundred yards or so cranes that rent the clouds and defied the law of gravity were continually swinging bricks and marble into the upper layers of the air. Violets were on sale at every corner, and the atmosphere was impregnated with an intoxicating perfume of methelated spirits. Presently he arrived at an immense arched façade bearing principally the legend 'Tea,' and he saw within hundreds of persons sipping tea; and next to that was another arched façade bearing principally the word 'Tea,' and he saw within more hundreds sipping tea; and then another; and then suddenly he came to an open circular place that seemed vaguely familiar.

'By Jove!' he said. 'This is Piccadilly Circus!'

And just at that moment, over a narrow doorway, he perceived the image of a green tree, and the words, 'The Elm Tree.' It was the entrance to the Elm Tree Tea Rooms, so well spoken of in the 'Telegraph.' In certain ways he was a man of advanced and humane ideas, and the thought of delicately nurtured needy gentlewomen bravely battling with the world instead of starving as they used to starve in the past appealed to his chivalry. He determined to assist them by taking tea in the advertised drawing-room. Gathering together his courage, he penetrated into a corridor lighted by pink electricity, and then up pink stairs. A pink door stopped him at last. It might have hid mysterious and questionable things, but it said laconically 'Push,' and he courageously pushed. . . . He was in a kind of boudoir thickly populated with tables and chairs. The swift transmigration from the blatant street to a drawing-room had a startling effect on him: it caused him to whip off his hat as though his hat had been red hot. Except for two tall elegant creatures who stood together at the other end of the boudoir, the chairs and tables had the place to themselves. He was about to stammer an excuse and fly, when one of the gentlewomen turned her eye on him for a moment, and so he sat down. The gentlewomen then resumed their conversation. He glanced cautiously about him. Elm trees, firmly rooted in a border of Indian matting, grew round all the walls in exotic profusion, and their topmost branches splashed over on to the ceiling. A card on the trunk of a tree, announcing curtly, 'Dogs not allowed,' seemed to enhearten him. After a pause one of the gentlewomen swam haughtily towards him and looked him between the eyes. She spoke no word, but her firm, austere glance said: 'Now, out with it, and see you behave yourself!'

He had been ready to smile chivalrously. But the smile was put to sudden death.

'Some tea, please,' he said faintly, and his intimidated tone said, 'If it isn't troubling you too much.'

'What do you want with it?' asked the gentlewoman abruptly, and as he was plainly at a loss she added, 'Crumpets or tea-cakes?'

'Tea-cake,' he replied, though he hated tea-cake. But he was afraid.

'You've escaped this time,' said the drapery of her muslins as she swam from his sight. 'But no nonsense while I'm away!'

When she sternly and mutely thrust the refection before him, he found that everything on the table except the tea-cakes and the spoon was growing elm trees.

After one cup and one slice, when the tea had become stewed and undrinkable, and the tea-cake a material suitable for the manufacture of shooting-boots, he resumed, at any rate partially, his presence of mind, and remembered that he had done nothing positively criminal in entering the boudoir or drawing-room and requesting food in return for money. Besides, the gentlewomen were now pretending to each other that he did not exist, and no other rash persons had been driven by hunger into the virgin forest of elm trees. He began to meditate, and his meditations, taking – for him – an unusual turn, caused him surreptitiously to examine Henry Leek's pocket-book (previously only known to him by sight). He had not for many years troubled himself concerning money, but the discovery that, when he had paid for the deposit of luggage at the cloak-room, a solitary sovereign rested in the pocket of Leek's trousers, had suggested to him that it would be advisable sooner or later to consider the financial aspect of existence.

There were two bank-notes for ten pounds each in Leek's pocket-book; also five French bank-notes for a thousand francs each, and a number of Italian bank-notes of small denominations: the equivalent of two hundred and thirty pounds altogether, not counting a folding inch-rule, some postage stamps, and a photograph of a pleasant-faced woman of forty or so. This sum seemed neither vast nor insignificant to Priam Farll. It seemed to him merely a tangible something which would enable him to banish the fiscal question from his mind for an indefinite period. He scarcely even troubled to wonder what Leek was doing with over two years of Leek's income in his pocket-book. He knew, or at least he with certainty guessed, that Leek had been a rascal. Still, he had had a sort of grim, cynical affection for Leek. And the thought that Leek would never again shave him, nor tell him in accents that brooked no delay that his hair must be cut, nor register his luggage and secure his seat in long-distance expresses, filled him with very real melancholy. He did not feel sorry for Leek, nor say to himself 'Poor Leek!' Nobody who had had the advantage of Leek's acquaintance would have said 'Poor Leek!' For Leek's greatest speciality had always been the speciality of looking after Leek, and wherever Leek might be it was a surety that Leek's interests would not suffer. Therefore Priam Farll's pity was mainly self-centred.

And though his dignity had been considerably damaged during the final moments at Selwood Terrace, there was matter for congratulation. The doctor, for instance, had shaken hands with him at parting; had shaken hands openly, in the presence of Duncan Farll; a flattering tribute to his personality. But the chief of Priam Farll's satisfactions in that desolate hour was that he had suppressed himself, that for the world he existed no more. I shall admit frankly that this satisfaction nearly outweighed his grief. He sighed – and it was a sigh of tremendous relief. For now, by a miracle, he would be free from the menace of Lady Sophia Entwistle. Looking back in calmness at the still recent Entwistle episode in Paris – the real originating cause of his sudden flight to London – he was staggered by his latent capacity for downright, impulsive foolishness. Like all shy people he had fits of amazing audacity – and his recklessness usually took the form of making himself agreeable to women whom he encountered in travel (he was much less shy with women than with men). But to propose marriage to a weather-beaten haunter of hotels like Lady Sophia Entwistle, and to reveal his identity to her and to allow her to accept his proposal – the thing had been unimaginably inept!

And now he was free, for he was dead.

He was conscious of a chill in the spine as he dwelt on the awful fate which he had escaped. He, a man of fifty, a man of set habits, a man habituated to the liberty of the wild stag, to bow his proud neck under the solid footwear of Lady Sophia Entwistle!

Yes, there was most decidedly a silver lining to the dark cloud of Leek's translation to another sphere of activity.

In replacing the pocket-book his hand encountered the letter which had arrived for Leek in the morning. Arguing with himself whether he ought to open it, he opened it. It ran: 'Dear Mr Leek, I am so glad to have your letter, and I think the photograph is most gentlemanly. But I do wish you would not write with a typewriter. You don't know how this affects a woman, or you wouldn't do it. However, I shall be so glad to meet you now, as you suggest. Suppose we go to Maskelyne and Cook's together to-morrow afternoon (Saturday). You know it isn't the Egyptian Hall any more. It is in St George's Hall, I think. But you will see it in the 'Telegraph'; also the time. I will be there when the doors open. You will recognize me from my photograph; but I shall wear red roses in my hat. So *au revoir* for the present. Yours sincerely, Alice Challice. P.S. – There are always a lot of dark parts at Maskelyne and Cook's. I must ask you to behave as a gentleman should. Excuse me. I merely mention it in case. – A.C.'

Infamous Leek! Here was at any rate one explanation of a mysterious little type-writer which the valet had always carried, but which Priam had left at Selwood Terrace.

Priam glanced at the photograph in the pocket-book: and also, strange to say, at the 'Telegraph.'

A lady with three children burst into the drawing-room, and instantly occupied the whole of it; the children cried 'Mathaw!' 'Mathah!' 'Mathaw!' in shrill tones of varied joy. As one of the gentlewomen passed near him, he asked modestly –

'How much, please?'

She dropped a flake of paper on to his table without arresting her course, and said warningly –

'You pay at the desk.'

When he hit on the desk, which was hidden behind a screen of elm trees, he had to face a true aristocrat – and not in muslins, either. If the others were the daughters of earls, this was the authentic countess in a tea-gown.

He put down Leek's sovereign.

'Haven't you anything smaller?' snapped the countess.

'I'm sorry I haven't,' he replied.

She picked up the sovereign scornfully, and turned it over.

'It's very awkward,' she muttered.

Then she unlocked two drawers, and unwillingly gave him eighteen and sixpence in silver and copper, without another word and without looking at him.

'Thank you,' said he, pocketing it nervously.

And amid reiterated cries of 'Mathah!' 'Mathaw!' 'Mathah!' he hurried away, unregarded, unregretted, splendidly repudiated by these delicate refined creatures who were struggling for a livelihood in a great city.

ALICE CHALLICE

'I suppose you are Mr Leek, aren't you?' a woman greeted him as he stood vaguely hesitant outside St George's Hall-,watching the afternoon audience emerge. He started back, as though the woman with her trace of Cockney accent had presented a revolver at his head. He was very much afraid. It may reasonably be asked what he was doing up at St George's Hall. The answer to this most natural question touches the deepest springs of human conduct. There were two men in Priam Farll. One was the shy man, who had long ago persuaded himself that he actually preferred not to mix with his kind, and had made a virtue of his cowardice. The other was a doggish, devil-may-care fellow who loved dashing adventures and had a perfect passion for free intercourse with the entire human race. No. 2 would often lead No. 1 unsuspectingly forward to a difficult situation from which No. 1, though angry and uncomfortable, could not retire.

Thus it was No. 2 who with the most casual air had wandered up Regent Street, drawn by the slender chance of meeting a woman with red roses in her hat; and it was No. 1 who had to pay the penalty. Nobody could have been more astonished than No. 2 at the fulfilment of No. 2's secret yearning for novelty. But the innocent sincerity of No 2's astonishment gave no aid to No. 1.

Farll raised his hat, and at the same moment perceived the roses. He might have denied the name of Leek and fled, but he did not. Though his left leg was ready to run, his right would not stir.

Then he was shaking hands with her. But how had she identified him?

'I didn't really expect you,' said the lady, always with a slight Cockney accent. 'But I thought how silly it would be for me to miss the vanishing trick just because you couldn't come. So in I went, by myself.'

'Why didn't you expect me?' he asked diffidently.

'Well,' she said, 'Mr Farll being dead, I knew you'd have a lot to do, besides being upset like.'

'Oh yes,' he said quickly, feeling that he must be more careful; for he had quite forgotten that Mr Farll was dead. 'How did you know?'

'How did I know!' she cried. 'Well, I like that! Look anywhere! It's all over London, has been these six hours.' She pointed to a ragged man who was wearing an orange-coloured placard by way of apron. On the placard was printed in large black letters: 'Sudden death of Priam Farll in London. Special Memoir.' Other ragged men, also wearing aprons, but of different colours, similarly proclaimed by their attire that Priam Farll was dead. And people crowding out of St George's Hall were continually buying newspapers from these middlemen of tidings.

He blushed. It was singular that he could have walked even half an hour in Central London without noticing that his own name flew in the summer breeze of every street. But so it had been. He was that sort of man. Now he understood how Duncan Farll had descended upon Selwood Terrace.

'You don't mean to say you didn't *see* those posters?' she demanded.

'I didn't,' he said simply.

'That shows how you must have been thinking!' said she. 'Was he a good master?'

'Yes, very good,' said Priam Farll with conviction.

'I see you're not in mourning.'

'No. That is — '

'I don't hold with mourning myself,' she proceeded. 'They say it's to show respect. But it seems to me that if you can't show your respect without a pair of black gloves that the dye's always coming off . . . I don't know what you think, but I never did hold with mourning. It's grumbling against Providence too! Not but what I think there's a good deal too much talk about Providence. I don't know what you think, but — '

'I quite agree with you,' he said, with a warm, generous smile which sometimes rushed up and transformed his face before he was aware of the occurrence.

And she smiled also, gazing at him half confidentially. She was a little woman, stoutish – indeed, stout; puffy red cheeks; a too remarkable white cotton blouse; and a crimson skirt that hung unevenly; grey cotton gloves; a green sunshade; on the top of all this the black hat with red roses. The photograph in Leek's pocket-book must have been taken in the past. She looked quite forty-five, whereas the photograph indicated thirty-nine and a fraction. He gazed down at her protectively, with a good-natured, appreciative condescension.

'I suppose you'll have to be going back again soon, to arrange things like,' she said. It was always she who kept the conversation afloat.

'No,' he said. 'I've finished there. They've dismissed me.'

'Who have?'

'The relatives.'

'Why?'

He shook his head.

'I hope you made them pay you your month,' said she firmly.

He was glad to be able to give a satisfactory answer.

After a pause she resumed bravely –

'So Mr Farll was one of these artists! At least so I see according to the paper.'

He nodded.

'It's a very funny business,' she said. 'But I suppose there's some of them make quite a nice income out of it. *You* ought to know about that, being in it, as it were.'

Never in his life had he conversed on such terms with such a person as Mrs Alice Challice. She was in every way a novelty for him – in clothes, manners, accent, deportment, outlook on the world and on paint. He had heard and read of such beings as Mrs Alice Challice, and now he was in direct contact with one of them. The whole affair struck him as excessively odd, as a mad escapade on his part. Wisdom in him deemed it ridiculous to prolong the encounter, but shy folly could not break loose. Moreover, she possessed the charm of her novelty; and there was that in her which challenged the male in him.

'Well,' she said, 'I suppose we can't stand here for ever!'

The crowd had frittered itself away, and an attendant was closing and locking the doors of St George's Hall. He coughed.

'It's a pity it's Saturday and all the shops closed. But anyhow, suppose we walk along Oxford Street all the same? Shall we?' This from her.

'By all means.'

'Now there's one thing I should like to say,' she murmured with a calm smile as they moved off. 'You've no occasion to be shy with me. There's no call for it. I'm just as you see me.'

'Shy!' he exclaimed, genuinely surprised. 'Do I seem shy to you?' He thought he had been magnificently doggish.

'Oh, well,' she said. 'That's all right, then, if you *aren't*. I should take it as a poor compliment, being shy with me. Where do you think we can have a good talk? I'm free for the evening. I don't know about you.'

Her eyes questioned his.

NO GRATUITIES

At a later hour, they were entering, side by side, a glittering establishment whose interior seemed to be walled chiefly in bevelled glass, so that everywhere the curious observer saw himself and twisted fractions of himself. The glass was relieved at frequent intervals by elaborate enamelled signs which repeated, 'No gratuities.' It seemed that the directors of the establishment wished to make perfectly clear to visitors that whatever else they might find, they must on no account expect gratuities.

'I have always wanted to come here,' said Mrs Challice vivaciously, glancing up at Priam Farll's modest middle-aged face.

Then after they had successfully passed through a preliminary pair of bevelled portals, a huge man dressed like a
policeman, and achieving a very successful imitation of a
policeman, stretched out his hand, and stopped them.

'In line, please,' he said.

'I thought it was a restaurant, not a theatre,' Priam whispered to Mrs Challice.

'So it is a restaurant,' said his companion. 'But I hear they're
obliged to do like this because there's always such a crowd. It's
very 'andsome, isn't it?'

He agreed that it was. He felt that London had got a long
way in front of him, and that he would have to hurry a great
deal before he could catch it up.

At length another imitation of a policeman opened more
doors, and, with other sinners, they were released from
purgatory into a clattering paradise, which again offered
everything save gratuities. They were conducted to a small
table full of dirty plates and empty glasses in a corner of the
vast and lofty saloon. A man in evening dress whose eye said,
'Now mind, no insulting gratuities!' rushed past the table and
in one deft amazing gesture swept off the whole of its contents
and was gone with them. It was an astounding feat, and when
Priam recovered from his amazement he fell into another
amazement on discovering that by some magic means the man
in evening dress had insinuated a gold-charactered menu into
his hands. This menu was exceedingly long – it comprised
everything except gratuities – and, evidently knowing from
experience that it was not a document to be perused and
exhausted in five minutes, the man in evening dress took care
not to interrupt the studies of Priam Farll and Alice Challice
during a full quarter of an hour. Then he returned like a bolt,
put them through an examination in the menu, and fled, and
when he was gone they saw that the table was set with a clean
cloth and instruments and empty glasses. A band thereupon
burst into gay strains, like the band at a music-hall after
something very difficult on the horizontal bar. And it played
louder and louder; and as it played louder, so the people talked
louder. And the crash of cymbals mingled with the clash of
plates, and the altercations of knives and forks with the shrill
accents of chatterers determined to be heard. And men in

evening dress (a costume which seemed to be forbidden to sitters at tables) flitted to and fro with inconceivable rapidity, austere, pre-occupied conjurors. And from every marble wall, bevelled mirror, and Doric column, there spoke silently but insistently the haunting legend, 'No gratuities.'

Thus Priam Farll began his first public meal in modern London. He knew the hotels, he knew the restaurants, of half a dozen countries, but he had never been so overwhelmed as he was here. Remembering London as a city of wooden chop-houses, he could scarcely eat for the thoughts that surged through his brain.

'Isn't it amusing?' said Mrs Challice benignantly over a glass of lager, 'I'm so glad you brought me here. I've always wanted to come.'

And then, a few minutes afterwards, she was saying, against the immense din –

'You know, I've been thinking for years of getting married again. And if you really *are* thinking of getting married, what are you to do? You may sit in a chair and wait till eggs are sixpence a dozen, and you'll be no nearer. You must do something. And what is there except a matrimonial agency? I say – what's the matter with a matrimonial agency, anyhow? If you want to get married, you want to get married, and it's no use pretending you don't. I do hate pretending, I do. No shame in wanting to get married, is there? I think a matrimonial agency is a very good, useful thing. They say you're swindled. Well, those that are deserve to be. You can be swindled without a matrimonial agency, seems to me. Not that I've never been. Plain common-sense people never are. No, if you ask me, matrimonial agencies are the most sensible things – after dress-shields – that's ever been invented. And I'm sure if anything comes of this, I shall pay the fees with the greatest pleasure. Now don't you agree with me?'

The whole mystery stood explained.

'Absolutely!' he said.

And felt the skin creeping in the small of his back.

CHAPTER III

THE PHOTOGRAPH

From the moment of Mrs Challice's remarks in favour of
matrimonial agencies Priam Farll's existence became a torture
to him. She was what he had always been accustomed to think
of as 'a very decent woman'; but really . . . ! The sentence is
not finished because Priam never finished it in his own mind.
Fifty times he conducted the sentence as far as 'really,' and
there it dissolved into an uncomfortable cloud.

'I suppose we shall have to be going,' said she, when her ice
had been eaten and his had melted.

'Yes,' said he, and added to himself, 'But where?'

However, it would be a relief to get out of the restaurant,
and he called for the bill.

While they were waiting for the bill the situation grew more
strained. Priam was aware of a desire to fling down sovereigns
on the table and rush wildly away. Even Mrs Challice,
vaguely feeling this, had a difficulty in conversing.

'You *are* like your photograph!' she remarked, glancing at
his face, which – it should be said – had very much changed
within half an hour. He had a face capable of a hundred
expressions per day. His present expression was one of his
anxious expressions, medium in degree. It can be figured in
the mask of a person who is locked up in an iron strong-room,
and, feeling ill at ease, notices that the walls are getting red-hot
at the corners.

'Like my photograph?' he exclaimed, astonished that he
should resemble Leek's photograph.

'Yes,' she asseverated stoutly. 'I knew you at once. Especially by the nose.'

'Have you got it here?' he asked, interested to see what
portrait of Leek had a nose like his own.

And she pulled out of her handbag a photograph, not of
Leek, but of Priam Farll. It was an unmounted print of a
negative which he and Leek had taken together for the purpose
of a pose in a picture, and it had decidedly a distinguished
appearance. But why should Leek dispatch photographs of his

master to strange ladies introduced through a matrimonial agency? Priam Farll could not imagine – unless it was from sheer unscrupulous, careless bounce.

She gazed at the portrait with obvious joy.

'Now, candidly, don't *you* think it's very, very good?' she demanded.

'I suppose it is,' he agreed. He would probably have given two hundred pounds for the courage to explain to her in a few well-chosen words that there had been a vast mistake, a huge impulsive indiscretion. But two hundred thousand pounds would not have bought that courage.

'I love it,' she ejaculated fervently – with heat, and yet so nicely! And she returned the photograph to her little bag.

She lowered her voice.

'You haven't told me whether you were ever married. I've been waiting for that.'

He blushed. She was disconcertingly personal.

'No,' he said.

'And you've always lived like that, alone like; no home; travelling about; no one to look after you properly?' There was distress in her voice.

He nodded. 'One gets accustomed to it.'

'Oh yes,' she said. 'I can understand that.'

'No responsibilities,' he added.

'No. I can understand all that.' Then she hesitated. 'But I do feel sorry for you . . . all these years!'

And her eyes were moist, and her tone was so sincere that Priam Farll found it quite remarkably affecting. Of course she was talking about Henry Leek, the humble valet, and not about Leek's illustrious master. But Priam saw no difference between his lot and that of Leek. He felt that there was no essential difference, and that, despite Leek's multiple perfections as a valet, he never had been looked after – properly.

Her voice made him feel just as sorry for himself as she was sorry for him; it made him feel that she had a kind heart, and that a kind heart was the only thing on earth that really mattered. Ah! If Lady Sophia Entwistle had spoken to him in such accents . . . !

The bill came. It was so small that he was ashamed to pay it. The suppression of gratuities enabled the purchase of a

complete dinner for about the same price as a thimbleful of tea
and ten drachms of cake a few yards away. Happily the
monarch, foreseeing his shame, had arranged a peculiar
method of payment through a little hole, where the receiver
could see nothing but his blushing hands. As for the conjurers
in evening dress, they apparently never soiled themselves by
contact with specie.

Outside on the pavement, he was at a loss what to do. You
see, he was entirely unfamiliar with Mrs Challice's code of
etiquette.

'Would you care to go to the Alhambra or somewhere?' he
suggested, having a notion that this was the correct thing to
say to a lady whose presence near you was directly due to her
desire for marriage.

'It's very good of you,' said she. 'But I'm sure you only say
it out of kindness – because you're a gentleman. It wouldn't be
quite nice for you to go to a music-hall to-night. I know I said
I was free for the evening, but I wasn't thinking. It wasn't a
hint – no, truly! I think I shall go home – and perhaps some
other — '

'I shall see you home,' said he quickly. Impulsive, again!

'Would you really like to? Can you?' In the bluish glare of
an electricity that made the street whiter than day, she
blushed. Yes, she blushed like a girl.

She led him up a side-street where was a kind of railway
station unfamiliar to Priam Farll's experience, tiled like a
butcher's shop and as clean as Holland. Under her direction he
took tickets for a station whose name he had never heard of,
and then they passed through steel railings which clacked
behind them into a sort of safe deposit, from which the only
emergence was a long dim tunnel. Painted hands, pointing to
the mysterious word 'lifts,' waved you onwards down this
tunnel. 'Hurry up, please,' came a voice out of the spectral
gloom. Mrs Challice thereupon ran. Now up the tunnel,
opposing all human progress, there blew a steady trade-wind
of tremendous force. Immediately Priam began to run the
trade-wind removed his hat, which sailed buoyantly back
towards the street. He was after it like a youth of twenty, and
he recaptured it. But when he reached the extremity of the
tunnel his amazed eyes saw nothing but a great cage of human

animals pressed tightly together behind bars. There was a click, and the whole cage sank from his sight into the earth.

He felt that there was more than he had dreamt of in the city of miracles. In a couple of minutes another cage rose into the tunnel at a different point, vomited its captives, and descended swiftly again with Priam and many others, and threw him and the rest out into a white mine consisting of numberless galleries. He ran about these interminable galleries underneath London at the bidding of painted hands, for a considerable time and occasionally magic trains without engines swept across his vision. But he could not find even the spirit of Mrs Alice Challice in this nether world.

THE NEST

On letter-paper headed 'Grand Babylon Hotel, London,' he was writing, in a disguised backward hand, a note to the following effect: 'Duncan Farll, Esq. Sir, – If any letters or telegrams arrive for me at Selwood Terrace, be good enough to have them forwarded to me at once to the above address. – Yours truly, H. Leek.' It cost him something to sign the name of the dead man; but he instinctively guessed that Duncan Farll might be a sieve which (owing to its legal-mindedness) would easily get clogged up even by a slight suspicion. Hence, in order to be sure of receiving a possible letter or telegram from Mrs Challice, he must openly label himself as Henry Leek. He had lost Mrs Challice; there was no address on her letter; he only knew that she lived at or near Putney, and the sole hope of finding her again lay in the fact that she had the Selwood Terrace address. He wanted to find her again; he desired that ardently, if merely to explain to her that their separation was due to a sudden caprice of his hat, and that he had searched for her everywhere in the mine, anxiously, desperately. She would surely not imagine that he had slipped away from her on purpose? No! And yet, if incapable of such an enormity, why had she not waited for him on one of the platforms? However, he hoped for the best. The best was a telegram; the second-best a letter. On receipt of which he would fly to her to explain. . . . And besides, he wanted to see her – simply. Her answer to his suggestion of a music-hall, and the tone of it, had impressed him. And her remark, 'I do feel so sorry for you all these years,' had – well, somewhat changed his whole outlook on life. Yes, he wanted to see her in order to satisfy himself that he had her respect. A woman impossible socially, a woman with strange habits and tricks of manner (no doubt there were millions such); but a woman whose respect one would not forfeit without a struggle!

He had been pushed to an extremity, forced to act with swiftness, upon losing her. And he had done the thing that comes most naturally to a life-long traveller. He had driven to the best hotel in the town. (He had seen in a flash that the idea of inhabiting any private hotel whatever was a silly idea.) And now he was in a large bedroom overlooking the Thames – a chamber with a writing-desk, a sofa, five electric lights, two easy chairs, a telephone, electric bells, and a massive oak door with a lock and a key in the lock; in short, his castle! An enterprise of some daring to storm the castle: but he had stormed it. He had registered under the name of Leek, a name sufficiently common not to excite remark, and the floor-valet had proved to be an admirable young man. He trusted to the floor-valet and to the telephone for avoiding any rough contact with the world. He felt comparatively safe now; the entire enormous hotel was a nest for his shyness, a conspiracy to keep him in cotton-wool. He was an autocratic number, absolute ruler over Room 331, and with the right to command the almost limitless resources of the Grand Babylon for his own private ends.

As he sealed the envelope he touched a bell.

The valet entered.

'You've got the evening papers?' asked Priam Farll.

'Yes, sir.' The valet put a pile of papers respectfully on the desk.

'All of them?'

'Yes, sir.'

'Thanks. Well, it's not too late to have a messenger, is it?'

'Oh *no*, sir.' ('"Too late" in the Grand Babylon, oh Czar!' said the valet's shocked tone.)

'Then please get a messenger to take this letter, at once.'

'In a cab, sir?'

'Yes, in a cab. I don't know whether there will be an answer. He will see. Then let him call at the cloak-room at South Kensington Station and get my luggage. Here's the ticket.'

'Thank you, sir.'

'I can rely on you to see that he goes at once?'

'You can, sir,' said the valet, in such accents as carry absolute conviction.

'Thank you. That will do, I think.'

The man retired, and the door was closed by an expert in closing doors, one who had devoted his life to the perfection of detail in valetry.

FAME

He lay on the sofa at the foot of the bed, with all illumination extinguished save one crimson-shaded light immediately above him. The evening papers – white, green, rose, cream, and yellow – shared his couch. He was about to glance at the obituaries; to glance at them in a careless, condescending way, just to see the *sort* of thing that journalists had written of him. He knew the value of obituaries; he had often smiled at them. He knew also the exceeding fatuity of art criticism, which did not cause him even to smile, being simply a bore. He recollected, further, that he was not the first man to read his own obituary; the adventure had happened to others; and he could recall how, on his having heard that owing to an error it had happened to the great So-and-so, he, in his quality of philosopher, had instantly decided what frame of mind the great So-and-so ought to have assumed for the perusal of his biography. He carefully and deliberately adopted that frame of mind now. He thought of Marcus Aurelius on the futility of fame; he remembered his life-long attitude of gentle, tired scorn for the press; he reflected with wise modesty that in art nothing counts but the work itself, and that no quantity of inept chatter could possibly affect, for good or evil, his value such as it might be, to the world.

Then he began to open the papers.

The first glimpse of their contents made him jump. In fact, the physical result of it was quite extraordinary. His temperature increased. His heart became audible. His pulse quickened. And there was a tingling as far off as his toes. He had felt, in a dim, unacknowledged way, that he must be a pretty great painter. Of course his prices were notorious. And he had guessed, though vaguely, that he was the object of widespread curiosity. But he had never compared himself with Titanic figures on the planet. It had always seemed to him that *his* renown was different from other renowns, less – somehow unreal and make-believe. He had never imaginatively grasped, despite prices and public inquisitiveness, that he too was one of the Titanic figures. He grasped it now. The aspect of the papers brought it home to him with tremendous force.

Special large type! Titles stretching across two columns! Black borders round the pages! 'Death of England's greatest painter.' 'Sudden death of Priam Farll.' 'Sad death of a great genius.' 'Puzzling career prematurely closed.' 'Europe in mourning.' 'Irreparable loss to the world's art.' 'It is with the most profound regret.' 'Our readers will be shocked.' 'The news will come as a personal blow to every lover of great painting.' So the papers went on, outvying each other in enthusiastic grief.

He ceased to be careless and condescending to them. The skin crept along his spine. There he lay, solitary, under the crimson glow, locked in his castle, human, with the outward semblance of a man like other men, and yet the cities of Europe were weeping for him. He heard them weeping. Every lover of great painting was under a sense of personal bereavement. The very voice of the world was hushed. After all, it was something to have done your best; after all, good stuff *was* appreciated by the mass of the race. The phenomenon presented by the evening papers was certainly prodigious, and prodigiously affecting. Mankind was unpleasantly stunned by the report of his decease. He forgot that Mrs Challice, for instance, had perfectly succeeded in hiding her grief for the irreparable loss, and that her questions about Priam Farll had been almost perfunctory. He forgot that he had witnessed absolutely no sign of overwhelming sorrow, or of any degree of sorrow, in the thoroughfares of the teeming capital, and that the hotels did not resound to sobbing. He knew only that all Europe was in mourning!

'I suppose I was rather wonderful – *am*, I mean' – he said to himself, dazed and happy. Yes, happy. 'The fact is, I've got so used to my own work that perhaps I don't think enough of it.' He said this as modestly as he could.

There was no question now of casually glancing at the obituaries. He could not miss a single line, a single word. He even regretted that the details of his life were so few and unimportant. It seemed to him that it was the business of the journalists to have known more, to have displayed more enterprise in acquiring information. Still, the tone was right. The fellows meant well, at any rate. His eyes encountered nothing but praise. Indeed the Press of London had yielded itself up to an encomiastic orgy. His modesty tried to say that this was slightly overdone; but his impartiality asked, 'Really, what *could* they say against me?' As a rule unmitigated praise was nauseous, but here they were undoubtedly genuine, the fellows; their sentences rang true!

Never in his life had he been so satisfied with the scheme of the universe! He was nearly consoled for the dissolution of Leek.

When, after continued reading, he came across a phrase which discreetly insinuated, apropos of the policeman and the penguins, that capriciousness in the choice of subject was perhaps a pose with him, the accusation hurt.

'Pose!' he inwardly exclaimed. 'What a lie! The man's an ass!'

And he resented the following remark which concluded a 'special memoir' extremely laudatory in matter and manner, by an expert whose books he had always respected: 'However, contemporary judgments are in the large majority of cases notoriously wrong, and it behoves us to remember this in choosing a niche for our idol. Time alone can settle the ultimate position of Priam Farll.'

Useless for his modesty to whisper to him that contemporary judgments *were* notoriously wrong. He did not like it. It disturbed him. There were exceptions to every rule. And if the connoisseur meant anything at all, he was simply stultifying the rest of the article. Time be d—d!

He had come nearly to the last line of the last obituary before he was finally ruffled. Most of the sheets, in excusing

the paucity of biographical detail, had remarked that Priam
Farll was utterly unknown to London society, of a retiring
disposition, hating publicity, a recluse, etc. The word 'recluse'
grated on his sensitiveness a little; but when the least important of the evening papers roundly asserted it to be notorious
that he was of extremely eccentric habits, he grew secretly
furious. Neither his modesty nor his philosophy was influen-
tial enough to restore him to complete calm.

Eccentric! He! What next? Eccentric, indeed!

Now, what conceivable justification — ?

THE RULING CLASSES

Between a quarter-past and half-past eleven he was seated
alone at a small table in the restaurant of the Grand Babylon.
He had had no news of Mrs Challice; she had not instantly
telegraphed to Selwood Terrace, as he had wildly hoped. But
in the boxes of Henry Leek, safely retrieved by the messenger
from South Kensington Station, he had discovered one of his
old dress-suits, not too old, and this dress-suit he had donned.
The desire to move about unknown in the well-clad world,
the world of the frequenters of costly hotels, the world to
which he was accustomed, had overtaken him. Moreover, he
felt hungry. Hence he had descended to the famous restaurant,
whose wide windows were flung open to the illuminated
majesty of the Thames Embankment. The pale cream room
was nearly full of expensive women, and expending men, and
silver-chained waiters whose skilled, noiseless, inhuman
attentions were remunerated at the rate of about fourpence a
minute. Music, the midnight food of love, floated scarce heard
through the tinted atmosphere. It was the best imitation of
Roman luxury that London could offer, and after Selwood
Terrace and the rackety palace of no gratuities, Priam Farll
enjoyed it as one enjoys home after strange climes.

Next to his table was an empty table, set for two, to which
were presently conducted, with due state, a young man, and a
magnificent woman whose youth was slipping off her
polished shoulders like a cloak. Priam Farll then overheard the
following conversation: –

Man: Well, what are you going to have?

Woman: But look here, little Charlie, you can't possibly afford to pay for this!

Man: Never said I could. It's the paper that pays. So go ahead.

Woman: Is Lord Nasing so keen as all that?

Man: It isn't Lord Nasing. It's our brand-new editor specially imported from Chicago.

Woman: Will he last?

Man: He'll last a hundred nights, say as long as the run of your piece. Then he'll get six months' screw and the boot.

Woman: How much is six months' screw?

Man: Three thousand.

Woman: Well, I can hardly earn that myself.

Man: Neither can I. But then, you see, we weren't born in Chicago.

Woman: I've been offered a thousand dollars a week to go there, anyhow.

Man: Why didn't you tell me that for the interview? I've spent two entire entr'actes in trying to get something interesting out of you, and there you go and keep a thing like that up your sleeve. It's not fair to an old and faithful admirer. I shall stick it in. Poulet chasseur?

Woman: Oh no! Couldn't dream of it. Didn't you know I was dieting? Nothing saucy. No sugar. No bread. No tea. Thanks to that I've lost nearly a stone in six months. You know I *was* getting enormous.

Man: Let me put *that* in, eh?

Woman: Just try, and see what happens to you!

Man: Well, shall we say a lettuce salad, and a Perrier and soda? I'm dieting, too.

Waiter: Lettuce salad, and a Perrier and soda? Yes, sir.

Woman: You aren't very gay.

Man: Gay! You don't know all the yearnings of my soul. Don't imagine that because I'm a special of the 'Record' I haven't got a soul.

Woman: I suppose you've been reading that book 'Omar Khayyám,' that every one's talking about. Isn't that what it's called?

Man: Has 'Omar Khayyám' reached the theatrical world? Well, there's no doubt the earth does move, after all.

Woman: A little more soda, please. And just a trifle less impudence. What book ought one to be reading, then?

Man: Socialism's the thing just now. Read Wells on Socialism. It'll be all over the theatrical world in a few years' time.

Woman: No fear! I can't bear Wells. He's always stirring up the dregs. I don't mind froth, but I do draw the line at dregs. What's the band playing? What have you been doing to-day? *Is* this lettuce? No, no! No bread. Didn't you hear me tell you?

Man: I've been busy with the Priam Farll affair.

Woman: Priam Farll?

Man: Yes. Painter. *You* know.

Woman: Oh yes. *Him*! I saw it on the posters. He's dead, it seems. Anything mysterious?

Man: You bet! Very odd! Frightfully rich, you know! Yet he died in a wretched hovel of a place down off the Fulham Road. And his valet's disappeared. We had the first news of the death through our arrangement with all the registrars' clerks in London. Nasing sent me off at once to write up the story.

Woman: Story?

Man: The particulars. We always call it a story in Fleet Street.

Woman: What a good name! Well, did you find out anything interesting?

Man: Not very much. I saw his cousin, Duncan Farll, a money-lending lawyer in Clement's Lane – he only heard of it because we telephoned to him. But the fellow would scarcely tell me anything at all.

Woman: Really! I do hope there's something terrible.

Man: Why?

Woman: So that I can go to the inquest or the police court or whatever it is. That's why I always keep friendly with magistrates. It's so frightfully thrilling, sitting on the bench with them.

Man: There won't be any inquest. But there's something queer in it. You see, Priam Farll was never in England. Always abroad; at those foreign hotels wandering up and down.

Woman (*after a pause*): I know.

Man: What do you know?

Woman: Will you promise not to chatter?

Man: Yes.

Woman: I met him once at an hotel at Ostend. He – well, he wanted most tremendously to paint my portrait. But I wouldn't let him.

Man: Why not?

Woman: If you knew what sort of man he was you wouldn't ask.

Man: Oh! But look here, I say! You must let me use that in my story. Tell me all about it.

Woman: Not for worlds.

Man: He – he made up to you?

Woman: Rather!

Priam Farll (*to himself*): What a bare-faced lie! Never was at Ostend in my life.

Man: Can't I use it if I don't print your name – just say, a distinguished actress.

Woman: Oh yes, you can do *that*. You might say, of the musical comedy stage.

Man: I will. I'll run something together. Trust me. Thanks awfully.

At this point a young and emaciated priest passed up the room.

Woman: Oh! Father Luke, is that you? Do come and sit here and be nice. This is Father Luke Widgery – Mr Docksey of the 'Record.'

Man: Delighted.

Priest: Delighted.

Woman: Now, Father Luke, I've just *got* to come to your sermon to-morrow. What's it about?

Priest: Modern vice.

Woman: How charming! I read the last one – it was lovely.

Priest: Unless you have a ticket you'll never be able to get in.

Woman: But I must get in. I'll come to the vestry door, if there is a vestry door at St Bede's.

Priest: It's impossible. You've no idea of the crush. And I've no favourites.

Woman: Oh yes, you have! You have me.

Priest: In my church, fashionable women must take their chance with the rest.

Woman: How horrid you are!

Priest: Perhaps. I may tell you, Miss Cohenson, that I've seen two duchesses standing at the back of the aisle of St Bede's, and glad to be there.

Woman: But *I* shan't flatter you by standing at the back of your aisle, and you needn't think it. Haven't I given you a box for a music-hall before now?

Priest: I only accepted the box as a matter of duty; it is part of my duty to go everywhere.

Man: Come with me, Miss Cohenson, I've got two tickets for the 'Record.'

Woman: Oh, so you do send seats to the Press?

Priest: The Press is different. Waiter, bring me half a bottle of Heidsieck.

Waiter: Half a bottle Heidsieck? Yes, sir.

Woman: Heidsieck. Well, I like that. *We're* dieting.

Priest: I don't like Heidsieck. But I'm dieting, too. It's my doctor's orders. Every night before retiring. It appears that my system needs it. Maria Lady Rowndell insists on giving me a hundred a year to pay for it. It is her own beautiful way of helping the good cause. Ice, please, waiter. I've just been seeing her to-night. She's staying here for the season. Saves her a lot of trouble. She's very much cut up about the death of Priam Farll, poor thing! So artistic, you know! The late Lord Rowndell had what is supposed to be the finest lot of Farlls in England.

Man: Did you ever meet Priam Farll, Father Luke?

Priest: Never. I understand he was most eccentric. I hate eccentricity. I once wrote to him to ask him if he would paint a Holy Family for St Bede's.

Man: And what did he reply?

Priest: He didn't reply. Considering that he wasn't even an R.A., I don't think that it was quite nice of him. However, Maria Lady Rowndell insists that he must be buried in Westminster Abbey. She asked me what I could do.

Woman: Buried in Westminster Abbey! I'd no idea he was so big as all that! Gracious!

Priest: I have the greatest confidence in Maria Lady Rowndell's taste, and certainly I bear no grudge. I may be able to arrange something. My uncle the Dean —

Man: Pardon me. I always understood that since you left the Church —

Priest: Since I joined the Church, you mean. There is but one.

Man: Church of England, I meant.

Priest: Ah!

Man: Since you left the Church of England, there had been a breach between the Dean and yourself.

Priest: Merely religious. Besides, my sister is the Dean's favourite niece. And I am her favourite brother. My sister takes much interest in art. She has just painted a really exquisite tea-cosy for me. Of course the Dean ultimately settles these questions of national funerals. Hence . . .

At this point the invisible orchestra began to play 'God save the King.'

Woman: Oh! What a bore!

Then nearly all the lights were extinguished.

Waiter: Please, gentlemen! Gentlemen, please!

Priest: You quite understand, Mr Docksey, that I merely gave these family details in order to substantiate my statement that I may be able to arrange something. By the way, if you would care to have a typescript of my sermon to-morrow for the 'Record,' you can have one by applying at the vestry.

Waiter: Please, gentlemen!

Man: So good of you. As regards the burial in Westminster Abbey, I think that the 'Record' will support the project. I say I *think*.

Priest: Maria Lady Rowndell will be grateful.

Five-sixths of the remaining lights went out, and the entire company followed them. In the foyer there was a prodigious crush of opera cloaks, silk hats, and cigars, all jostling together. News arrived from the Strand that the weather had turned to rain, and all the intellect of the Grand Babylon was centred upon the British climate, exactly as if the British climate had been the latest discovery of science. As the doors swung to and fro, the stridency of whistles, the throbbing of motor-cars, and the hoarse cries of inhabitants of box seats mingled strangely with the delicate babble of the interior. Then, lo! as by magic, the foyer was empty save for the denizens of the hotel who could produce evidence of identity. It had been proved to demonstration, for the sixth time that week, that in the metropolis of the greatest of Empires there is not one law for the rich and another for the poor.

Deeply affected by what he had overheard, Priam Farll rose in a lift and sought his bed. He perceived clearly that he had been among the governing classes of the realm.

CHAPTER IV

A SCOOP

Within less than twelve hours after that conversation between members of the governing classes at the Grand Babylon Hotel, Priam Farll heard the first deep-throated echoes of the voice of England on the question of his funeral. The voice of England issued on this occasion through the mouth of the 'Sunday News,' a newspaper which belonged to Lord Nasing, the proprietor of the 'Daily Record.' There was a column in the 'Sunday News,' partly concerning the meeting of Priam Farll and a celebrated star of the musical comedy stage at Ostend. There was also a leading article, in which it was made perfectly clear that England would stand shamed among the nations if she did not inter her greatest painter in Westminster Abbey. Only the article, instead of saying Westminster Abbey, said National Valhalla. It seemed to make a point of not mentioning Westminster Abbey by name, as though Westminster Abbey had been something not quite mentionable, such as a pair of trousers. The article ended with the word 'basilica,' and by the time you had reached this majestic substantive, you felt indeed, with the 'Sunday News,' that a National Valhalla without the remains of a Priam Farll inside it would be shocking, if not inconceivable.

Priam Farll was extremely disturbed.

On Monday morning the 'Daily Record' came nobly to the support of the 'Sunday News.' It had evidently spent its Sunday in collecting the opinions of a number of famous men – including three M.P.s, a banker, a Colonial premier, a K.C., a cricketer, and the President of the Royal Academy – as to whether the National Valhalla was or was not a suitable place for the repose of the remains of Priam Farll; and the unanimous reply was in the affirmative. Other newspapers expressed the same view. But there were opponents of the scheme. Some organs coldly inquired what Priam Farll had *done* for England, and particularly for the higher life of England. He had not been a moral painter like Hogarth or Sir Noel Paton, nor a worshipper of classic legend and beauty like the unique Leighton. He had openly scorned England. He had never lived in England. He had avoided the Royal Academy, honouring every country save his own. And was he such a great painter, after all? Was he anything but a clever dauber whose work had been forced into general admiration by the efforts of a small clique of eccentric admirers? Far be it from them, the organs, to decry a dead man, but the National Valhalla was the National Valhalla. . . . And so on.

The penny evening papers were pro-Farll, one of them furiously so. You gathered that if Priam Farll was not buried in Westminster Abbey the penny evening papers would, from mere disgust, wipe their boots on Dover cliffs, and quit England eternally for some land where art was understood. You gathered, by nightfall, that Fleet Street must be a scene of carnage, full of enthusiasts cutting each other's throats for the sake of the honour of art. However, no abnormal phenomenon was superficially observable in Fleet Street; nor was martial law proclaimed at the Arts Club in Dover Street. London was impassioned by the question of Farll's funeral; a few hours would decide if England was to be shamed among the nations: and yet the town seemed to pursue its jog-trot way exactly as usual. The Gaiety Theatre performed its celebrated nightly musical comedy, 'House Full'; and at Queen's Hall quite a large audience was collected to listen to a violinist aged twelve, who played like a man, though a little one, and whose services had been bought for seven years by a limited company.

The next morning the controversy was settled by one of the 'Daily Record's' characteristic 'scoops.' In the nature of the case, such controversies, if they are not settled quickly, settle themselves quickly; they cannot be prolonged. But it was the

'Daily Record' that settled this one. The 'Daily Record' came out with a copy of the will of Priam Farll, in which, after leaving a pound a week for life to his valet, Henry Leek, Priam Farll bequeathed the remainder of his fortune to the nation for the building and upkeep of a Gallery of Great Masters. Priam Farll's own collection of great masters, gradually made by him in that inexpensive manner which is possible only to the finest connoisseurs, was to form the nucleus of the Gallery. It comprised, said the 'Record,' several Rembrandts, a Velasquez, six Vermeers, a Giorgione, a Turner, a Charles, two Cromes, a Holbein. (After Charles the 'Record' put a note of interrogation, itself being uncertain of the name.) The pictures were in Paris – had been for many years. The leading idea of the Gallery was that nothing not absolutely first-class should be admitted to it. The testator attached two conditions to the bequests. One was that his own name should be inscribed nowhere in the building, and the other was that none of his own pictures should be admitted to the gallery. Was not this sublime? Was not this true British pride? Was not this magnificently unlike the ordinary benefactor of his country? The 'Record' was in a position to assert that Priam Farll's estate would amount to about a hundred and forty thousand pounds, in addition to the value of the pictures. After that, was anybody going to argue that he ought not to be buried in the National Valhalla, a philanthropist so royal and so proudly meek.

The opposition gave up.

Priam Farll grew more and more disturbed in his fortress at the Grand Babylon Hotel. He perfectly remembered making the will. He had made it about seventeen years before, after some champagne in Venice, in an hour of anger against some English criticisms of his work. Yes, English criticisms! It was his vanity that had prompted him to reply in that manner. Moreover, he was quite young then. He remembered the youthful glee with which he had appointed his next-of-kin, whoever they might be, executors and trustees of the will. He remembered his cruel joy in picturing their disgust at being compelled to carry out the terms of such a will. Often, since, he had meant to destroy the will; but carelessly he had always omitted to do so. And his collection and his fortune had continued to increase regularly and mightily, and now – well, there the thing was! Duncan Farll had found the will. And Duncan Farll would be the executor and trustee of that melodramatic testament.

He could not help smiling, serious as the situation was.

During that day the thing was settled; the authorities spoke; the word went forth. Priam Farll was to be buried in Westminster Abbey on the Thursday. The dignity of England among artistic nations had been saved, partly by the heroic efforts of the 'Daily Record,' and partly by the will, which proved that after all Priam Farll had had the highest interests of his country at heart.

COWARDICE

On the night between Thursday and Wednesday Priam Farll had not a moment of sleep. Whether it was the deep-throated voice of England that had spoken, or merely the voice of the Dean's favourite niece – so skilled in painting tea-cosies – the affair was excessively serious. For the nation was preparing to inter in the National Valhalla the remains of just Henry Leek! Priam's mind had often a sardonic turn; he was assuredly capable of strange caprices: but even he could not permit an error so gigantic to continue. The matter must be rectified, and instantly! And he alone could rectify it. The strain on his shyness would be awful, would be scarcely endurable. Nevertheless, he must act. Quite apart from other considerations, there was the consideration of that hundred and forty thousand pounds, which was his, and which he had not the slightest desire to leave to the British nation. And as for giving his beloved pictures to the race which adored Landseer, Edwin Long, and Leighton – the idea nauseated him.

He must go and see Duncan Farll! And explain! Yes, explain that he was not dead.

Then he had a vision of Duncan Farll's hard, stupid face, and impenetrable steel head; and of himself being kicked out of the house, or delivered over to a policeman, or in some subtler way unimaginably insulted. Could he confront Duncan Farll? Was a hundred and forty thousand pounds and the dignity of the British nation worth the bearding of Duncan Farll? No! His distaste for Duncan Farll amounted to more than a hundred and forty millions of pounds and the dignity of whole planets. He felt that he could never bring himself to meet Duncan Farll. Why, Duncan might shove him into a lunatic asylum, might . . . !

Still, he must act.

Then it was that occurred to him the brilliant notion of making a clean breast of it to the Dean. He had not the pleasure of the Dean's personal acquaintance. The Dean was an abstraction; certainly much more abstract than Priam Farll. He thought he could meet the Dean. A terrific enterprise, but he must accomplish it! After all, a Dean – what was it? Nothing but a man with a funny hat! And was not he himself Priam Farll, the authentic Priam Farll, vastly greater than any Dean?

He told the valet to buy black gloves, and a silk hat, size seven and a quarter, and to bring up a copy of 'Who's Who.' He hoped the valet would be dilatory in executing these commands. But the valet seemed to fulfil them by magic. Time flew so fast that (in a way of speaking) you could hardly see the fingers as they whirled round the clock. And almost before he knew where he was, two commissionaires were helping him into an auto-cab, and the terrific enterprise had begun. The auto-cab would easily have won the race for the Gordon-Bennett Cup. It was of about two hundred h.p., and it arrived in Dean's Yard in less time than a fluent speaker would take to say Jack Robinson. The rapidity of its flight was simply incredible.

'I'll keep you,' Priam Farll was going to say, as he descended, but he thought it would be more final to dismiss the machine; and so he dismissed it.

He rang the bell with frantic haste, lest he should run away ere he had rung it. And then his heart went thumping, and the perspiration damped the lovely lining of his new hat; and his legs trembled, literally!

He was in hell on the Dean's doorstep.

The door was opened by a man in livery of prelatical black, who eyed him inimically.

'Er— ' stammered Priam Farll, utterly flustered and craven. 'Is this Mr Parker's?'

Now Parker was not the Dean's name, and Priam knew that it was not. Parker was merely the first name that had come into Priam's cowardly head.

'No, it isn't,' said the flunkey, with censorious lips. 'It's the Dean's.'

'Oh, I beg pardon,' said Priam Farll. 'I thought it was Mr Parker's.'

And he departed.

Between the ringing of the bell and the flunkey's appearance, he had clearly seen what he was capable, and what he was incapable of doing. And the correction of England's error was among his incapacities. He could not face the Dean. He could not face any one. He was a poltroon in all these things; a poltroon. No use arguing! He could not do it.

'I thought it was Mr Parker's!' Good heavens! To what depths can a great artist fall.

That evening he received a cold letter from Duncan Farll, with a nave-ticket for the funeral. Duncan Farll did not venture to be sure that Mr Henry Leek would think it proper to attend his master's interment; but he enclosed a ticket. He also stated that the pound a week would be paid to him in due course. Lastly he stated that several newspaper representatives had demanded Mr Henry Leek's address, but he had not thought fit to gratify this curiosity.

Priam was glad of that.

'Well, I'm dashed!' he reflected, handling the ticket for the nave.

There it was, large, glossy, real as life.

IN THE VALHALLA

In the vast nave there were relatively few people – that is to say, a few hundreds, who had sufficient room to move easily to and fro under the eyes of the officials. Priam Farll had been admitted through the cloisters according to the direction printed on the ticket. In his nervous fancy, he imagined that everybody must be gazing at him suspiciously, but the fact was that he occupied the attention of no one at all. He was with the unprivileged, on the wrong side of the massive screen which separated the nave from the packed choir and transepts, and the unprivileged are never interested in themselves; it is the privileged who interest them. The organ was wafting a melody of Purcell to the fartherest limits of the Abbey. Round a roped space a few ecclesiastical uniforms kept watch over the ground that would be the tomb. The sunlight of noon beat and quivered in long lances through crimson and blue windows. Then the functionaries began to form an aisle among the spectators, and emotion grew tenser. The organ was silent for a moment, and when it recommenced its song the song was the supreme expression of human grief, the dirge of Chopin, wrapping the whole cathedral in heavy folds of sorrow. And as that appeal expired in the pulsating air, the fresh voices of little boys, sweeter even than grief, rose in the distance.

It was at this point that Priam Farll descried Lady Sophia Entwistle, a tall veiled figure in full mourning. She had come among the comparatively unprivileged to his funeral. Doubtless influence such as hers could have obtained her a seat in the transept, but she had preferred the secluded humility of the nave. She had come from Paris for his funeral! She was weeping for her affianced. She stood there, actually within ten yards of him. She had not caught sight of him, but she might do at any moment, and she was slowly approaching the spot where he trembled.

He fled, with nothing in his heart but resentment against her, she had not proposed to him; he had proposed to her. She had not thrown him aside; he had thrown her aside. He was not one of her mistakes; she was one of his mistakes. Not she, but he, had been capricious, impulsive, hasty. Yet he hated her. He genuinely thought she had sinned against him, and that she ought to be exterminated. He condemned her for all manner of things as to which she had had no choice; for instance, the irregularity of her teeth, and the hollow under her chin, and the little tricks of deportment which are always developed by a spinster as she reaches forty. He fled in terror of her. If she should have a glimpse of him, and should recognize him, the consequence would be absolutely disastrous – disastrous in every way; and a period of publicity would dawn for him such as he could not possibly contem-

plate either in cold blood or warm. He fled blindly, insinuating himself through the crowd, until he reached a grille in
which was a gate, ajar. His strange stare must have affrighted
the guardian of the gate, for the robed fellow stood away, and
Priam passed within the grille, where were winding steps,
which he mounted. Up the steps ran coils of fire-hose. He
heard the click of the gate as the attendant shut it, and he was
thankful for an escape. The steps led to the organ-loft, perched
on the top of the massive screen. The organist was seated
behind a half-drawn curtain, under shaded electric lights, and
on the ample platform, whose parapet overlooked the choir,
were two young men who whispered with the organist. None
of the three even glanced at Priam. Priam sat down on a
windsor chair fearfully, like an intruder, his face towards the
choir.

The whispers ceased; the organist's fingers began to move
over five rows of keys, and over scores of stops, while his feet
groped beneath, and Priam heard music, afar off. And close
behind him he heard rumblings, steamy vibrations, and, as it
were, sudden escapes of gas; and comprehended that these
were the hoarse responses of the 32 and 64 foot pipes, laid
horizontally along the roof of the screen, to the summoning
fingers of the organist. It was all uncanny, weird, super-
natural, demoniacal, if you will – it was part of the secret and
unsuspected mechanism of a vast emotional pageant and
spectacle. It unnerved Priam, especially when the organist, a
handsome youngish man with lustrous eyes, half turned and
winked at one of his companions.

The thrilling voices of the choristers grew louder, and as
they grew louder Priam Farll was conscious of unaccustomed
phenomena in his throat, which shut and opened of itself
convulsively. To divert his attention from his throat, he
partially rose from the windsor chair, and peeped over the
parapet of the screen into the choir, whose depths were
candle-lit and whose altitudes were capriciously bathed by the
intermittent splendours of the sun. High, high up in front of
him, at the summit of a precipice of stone, a little window, out
of the sunshine, burned sullenly in a gloom of complicated
perspectives. And far below, stretched round the pulpit and
disappearing among the forest of statuary in the transept, was

a floor consisting of the heads of the privileged – famous, renowned, notorious, by heredity, talent, enterprise, or hazard; he had read many of their names in the 'Daily Telegraph.' The voices of the choristers had become piercing in their beauty. Priam frankly stood up, and leaned over the parapet. Every gaze was turned to a point under him which he could not see. And then something swayed from beneath into the field of his vision. It was a tall cross borne by a beadle. In the wake of the cross there came to view gorgeous ecclesiastics in pairs, and then a robed man walking backwards and gesticulating in the manner of some important, excited official of the Salvation Army; and after this violet robe arrived the scarlet choristers, singing to the beat of his gesture. And then swung into view the coffin, covered with a heavy purple pall, and on the pall a single white cross; and the pall-bearers – great European names that had hurried out of the corners of Europe as at a peremptory mandate – with Duncan Farll to complete the tale.

Was it the coffin, or the richness of its pall, or the solitary whiteness of its cross of flowers, or the august authority of the bearers, that affected Priam Farll like a blow on the heart? Who knows? But the fact was that he could look no more; the scene was too much for him. Had he continued to look he would have burst uncontrollably into tears. It mattered not that the corpse of a common rascally valet lay under that pall; it mattered not that a grotesque error was being enacted; it mattered not whether the actuating spring of the immense affair was the Dean's water-colouring niece or the solemn deliberations of the Chapter; it mattered not that newspapers had ignobly misused the name and honour of art for their own advancement – the instant effect was overwhelmingly impressive. All that had been honest and sincere in the heart of England for a thousand years leapt mystically up and made it impossible that the effect should be other than overwhelmingly impressive. It was an effect beyond argument and reason: it was the magic flowering of centuries in a single moment, the awful sigh of a nation's secular soul. It took majesty and loveliness from the walls around it, and rendered them again tenfold. It left nothing common, neither the motives nor the littleness of men. In Priam's mind it gave dignity to Lady Sophia Entwistle, and profound tragedy to the death of Leek; it transformed even the gestures of the choir-leader into grave commands.

And all that was for him! He had brushed pigments on the cloth in a way of his own, nothing more, and the nation to which he had always denied artistic perceptions, the nation which he had always fiercely accused of sentimentality, was thus solemnizing his committal to the earth! Divine mystery of art! The large magnificence of England smote him! He had not suspected his own greatness, nor England's.

The music ceased. He chanced to look up at the little glooming window, perched out of reach of mankind. And the thought that the window had burned there, patiently and unexpectedly, for hundreds of years, like an anchorite above the river and town, somehow disturbed him so that he could not continue to look at it. Ineffable sadness of a mere window! And his eye fell – fell on the coffin of Henry Leek with its white cross, and the representatives of England's majesty standing beside it. And there was the end of Priam Farll's self-control. A pang like a pang of parturition itself seized him, and an issuing sob nearly ripped him in two. It was a loud sob, undisguised, unashamed, reverberating. Other sobs succeeded it. Priam Farll was in torture.

A NEW HAT

The organist vaulted over his seat, shocked by the outrage.

'You really mustn't make that noise,' whispered the organist.

Priam Farll shook him off.

The organist was apparently at a loss what to do.

'Who is it?' whispered one of the young men.

'Don't know him from Adam!' said the organist with conviction, and then to Priam Farll: 'Who are you? You've no right to be here. Who gave you permission to come up here?'

And the rending sobs continued to issue from the full-bodied ridiculous man of fifty, utterly careless of decorum.

'It's perfectly absurd!' whispered the youngster who had whispered before.

There had been a silence in the choir.

'Here! They're waiting for you!' whispered the other young man excitedly to the organist.

'By—!' whispered the alarmed organist, not stopping to say by what, but leaping like an acrobat back to his seat. His fingers and boots were at work instantly, and as he played he turned his head and whispered –

'Better fetch some one.'

One of the young men crept quickly and creakingly down the stairs. Fortunately the organ and choristers were now combined to overcome the sobbing, and they succeeded. Presently a powerful arm, hidden under a black cassock, was laid on Priam's shoulder. He hysterically tried to free himself, but he could not. The cassock and the two young men thrust him downwards. They all descended together, partly walking and partly falling. And then a door was opened, and Priam discovered himself in the unroofed air of the cloisters, without his hat, and breathing in gasps. His executioners were also breathing in gasps. They glared at him in triumphant menace, as though they had done something, which indeed they had, and as though they meant to do something more but could not quite decide what.

'Where's your ticket of admission?' demanded the cassock.

Priam fumbled for it, and could not find it.

'I must have lost it,' he said weakly.

'What's your name, anyhow?'

'Priam Farll,' said Priam Farll, without thinking.

'Off his nut, evidently!' murmured one of the young men contemptuously. 'Come on, Stan. Don't let's miss that anthem, for this cuss.' And off they both went.

Then a youthful policeman appeared, putting on his helmet as he quitted the fane.

'What's all this?' asked the policeman, in the assured tone of one who had the forces of the Empire behind him.

'He's been making a disturbance in the horgan loft,' said the cassock, 'and now he says his name's Priam Farll.'

'Oh!' said the policeman. 'Ho! And how did he get into the organ loft?'

'Don't arsk me,' answered the cassock. 'He ain't got no ticket.'

'Now then, out of it!' said the policeman, taking zealously hold of Priam.

'I'll thank you to leave me alone,' said Priam, rebelling with all the pride of his nature against this clutch of the law.

'Oh, you will, will you?' said the policeman. 'We'll see about that. We shall just see about that.'

And the policeman dragged Priam along the cloister to the muffled music of 'He will swallow up death in victory.' They had not thus proceeded very far when they met another policeman, an older policeman.

'What's all this?' demanded the older policeman.

'Drunk and disorderly in the Abbey!' said the younger.

'Will you come quietly?' the older policeman asked Priam, with a touch of commiseration.

'I'm not drunk,' said Priam fiercely; he was unversed in London, and unaware of the foolishness of reasoning with the watch-dogs of justice.

'Will you come quietly?' the older policeman repeated, this time without any touch of commiseration.

'Yes,' said Priam.

And he went quietly. Experience may teach with the rapidity of lightning.

'But where's my hat?' he added after a moment, instinctively stopping.

'Now then!' said the older policeman. 'Come *on*.'

He walked between them, striding. Just as they emerged into Dean's Yard, his left hand nervously exploring one of his pockets, on a sudden encountered a piece of cardboard.

'Here's my ticket,' he said. 'I thought I'd lost it. I've had nothing at all to drink, and you'd better let me go. The whole affair's a mistake.'

The procession halted, while the older policeman gazed fascinated at the official document.

'Henry Leek,' he read, deciphering the name.

'He's been a-telling every one as he's Priam Farll,' grumbled the younger policeman, looking over the other's shoulder.

'I've done no such thing,' said Priam promptly.

The elder carefully inspected the prisoner, and two little boys arrived and formed a crowd, which was immediately dispersed by a frown.

'He don't look as if he'd had 'ardly as much drink as 'ud
wash a 'bus, does he?' murmured the elder critically. The
younger, afraid of his senior, said nothing. 'Look here, Mr
Henry Leek,' the elder proceeded, 'do you know what I
should do if I was you? I should go and buy myself a new hat if
I was you, and quick too!'

Priam hastened away, and heard the senior say to the junior.
'He's a toff, that's what he is, and you're a fool. Have you
forgotten as you're on point duty?'

And such is the effect of a suggestion given under certain
circumstances by a man of authority, that Priam Farll went
straight along Victoria Street and at Sowter's famous one-
price hat-shop did in fact buy himself a new hat. He then
hailed a taximeter from the stand opposite the Army and
Navy Stores, and curtly gave the address of the Grand
Babylon Hotel. And when the cab was fairly at speed, and not
before, he abandoned himself to a fit of candid, unrestrained
cursing. He cursed largely and variously and shamelessly both
in English and in French. And he did not cease cursing. It was
a reaction which I do not care to characterize; but I will not
conceal that it occurred. The fit spent itself before he reached
the hotel, for most of Parliament Street was blocked for the
spectacular purposes of his funeral, and his driver had to seek
devious ways. The cursing over, he began to smooth his
plumes in detail. At the hotel, out of sheer nervousness, he
gave the cabman half a crown, which was preposterous.

Another cab drove up nearly at the exact instant of his
arrival. And, as a capping to the day, Mrs Alice Challice
stepped out of it.

CHAPTER V

ALICE ON HOTELS

She was wearing the same red roses.

'Oh!' she said, very quickly, pouring out the words generously from the inexhaustible mine of her good heart. 'I'm so

sorry I missed you Saturday night. I can't tell you how sorry I am. Of course it was all my fault. I oughtn't to have got into the lift without you. I ought to have waited. When I was in the lift I wanted to get out, but the lift-man was too quick for me. And then on the platforms— well, there was such a crowd it was useless! I knew it was useless. And you not having my address either! I wondered whatever you would think of me.'

'My dear lady,' he protested. 'I can assure you I blamed only myself. My hat blew off, and—'

'Did it now!' she took him up breathlessly. 'Well, all I want you to understand really is that I'm not one of those silly sort of women that go losing themselves. No. Such a thing's never happened to me before, and I shall take good care—'

She glanced round. He had paid both the cabmen, who were departing, and he and Mrs Alice Challice stood under the immense glass portico of the Grand Babylon, exposed to the raking stare of two commissionaires.

'So you *are* staying here!' she said, as if laying hold of a fact which she had hitherto hesitated to touch.

'Yes,' he said. 'Won't you come in?'

He took her into the rich gloom of the Grand Babylon dashingly, fighting with the demon of shyness and beating it off with great loss. They sat down in a corner of the principal foyer, where a few electric lights drew attention to empty fauteuils and the blossoms of the Aubasson carpet. The world was at lunch.

'And a fine time I had getting your address!' said she. 'Of course I wrote at once to Selwood Terrace, as soon as I got home, but I had the wrong number somehow, and I kept waiting and waiting for an answer, and the only answer I received was the returned letter. I knew I'd got the street right, and I said, 'I'll find that house if I have to ring every bell in Selwood Terrace, yes, and knock every knocker.' Well, I did find it, and then they wouldn't *give* me your address. They said "letters would be forwarded," if you please. But I wasn't going to have any more letter business, no, thank you! So I said I wouldn't go without the address. It was Mr Duncan Farll's clerk that I saw. He's living there for the time being. A very nice young man. We got quite friendly. It seems Mr Duncan Farll *was* in a state when he found the will. The young man did say that he broke a typewriter all to pieces. But the funeral being in Westminster Abbey consoled him. It wouldn't have consoled me – no, not it! However, he's very rich himself, so that doesn't matter. The young man said if I'd call again he'd ask his master if he might give me your address. A rare fuss over an address, thought I to myself. But there! Lawyers! So I called again, and he gave it me. I could have come yesterday. I very nearly wrote last night. But I thought on the whole I'd better wait till the funeral was over. I thought it would be nicer. It's over now, I suppose?'

'Yes,' said Priam Farll.

She smiled at him with grave sympathy, comfortably and sensibly. 'And right down relieved you must be!' she murmured. 'It must have been very trying for you.'

'In a way,' he answered hesitatingly, 'it was.'

Taking off her gloves, she glanced round about her, as a thief must glance before opening the door, and then, leaning suddenly towards him, she put her hand to his neck and touched his collar. 'No, no!' she said. 'Let me do it. It's unbuttoned; the necktie was holding it in place, but it's quite loose now. There! I can do it. I see you've got two funny moles on your neck, close together. How lucky! That's it!' A final pat!

Now, no woman had ever patted Priam Farll's necktie before, much less buttoned his collar, and still much less referred to the two little moles, one hirsute, the other hairless, which the collar hid – when it was properly buttoned! The experience was startling for him in the extreme. It might have made him very angry, had the hands of Mrs Challice not been – well, nurse's hands, soft hands, persuasive hands, hands that could practise impossible audacities with impunity. Imagine a woman, uninvited and unpermitted, arranging his collar and necktie for him in the largest public room of the Grand Babylon, and then talking about his little moles! It would have been unimaginable! Yet it happened. And moreover, he had not disliked it. She sat back in her chair as though she had done nothing in the least degree unusual.

'I can see you must have been very upset,' she said gently, 'though he *has* only left you a pound a week. Still, that's better than a bat in the eye with a burnt stick.'

A bat in the eye with a burnt stick reminded him vaguely of encounters with the police; otherwise it conveyed no meaning to his mind.

'I hope you haven't got to go on duty at once,' she said after a pause. 'Because you really do look as if you needed a rest, and a cup of tea or something of that. I'm quite ashamed to have come bothering you so soon.'

'Duty?' he questioned. 'What duty?'

'Why,' she exclaimed, 'haven't you got a new place?'

'New place!' he repeated after her. 'What do you mean?'

'Why, as valet.'

There was certainly danger in his tendency to forget that he was a valet. He collected himself.

'No,' he said, 'I haven't got a new place.'

'Then why are you staying here?' she cried. 'I thought you were simply here with a new master. Why are you staying here alone?'

'Oh,' he replied, abashed, 'it seemed a convenient place. It was just by chance that I came here.'

'Convenient place, indeed!' she said stoutly. 'I never heard of such a thing!'

He perceived that he had shocked her, pained her. He saw that some ingenious defence of himself was required; but he could find none. So he said, in his confusion –

'Suppose we go and have something to eat? I do want a bit of lunch, as you say, now I come to think of it. Will you?'

'What? Here?' she demanded apprehensively.

'Yes,' he said. 'Why not?'

'Well—!'

'Come along!' he said, with fine casualness, and conducted her to the eight swinging glass doors that led to the salle à manger of the Grand Babylon. At each pair of doors was a living statue of dignity in cloth of gold. She passed these statues without a sign of fear, but when she saw the room itself, steeped in a supra-genteel calm, full of gowns and hats and everything that you read about in the 'Lady's Pictorial,' and the pennoned mast of a barge crossing the windows at the other end, she stopped suddenly. And one of the lord mayors of the Grand Babylon, wearing a mayoral chain, who had started out to meet them, stopped also.

'No!' she said. 'I don't feel as if I could eat here. I really couldn't.'

'But why?'

'Well,' she said. 'I couldn't fancy it somehow. Can't we go somewhere else?'

'Certainly we can,' he agreed with an eagerness that was more than polite.

She thanked him with another of her comfortable sensible smiles – a smile that took all embarrassment out of the dilemma, as balm will take irritation from a wound. And gently she removed her hat and gown, and her gestures and speech, and her comfortableness from those august precincts. And they descended to the grill-room, which was relatively noisy, and where her roses were less conspicuous than the helmet of Navarre, and her frock found its sisters and cousins from far lands.

'I'm not much for these restaurants,' she said, over grilled kidneys.

'No?' he responded tentatively. 'I'm sorry. I thought the other night—'

'Oh yes,' she broke in, 'I was very glad to go, the other night, to that place, very glad. But, you see, I'd never been in a restaurant before.'

'Really?'

'No,' she said, 'and I felt as if I should like to try one. And the young lady at the post office had told me that *that* one was a splendid one. So it is. It's beautiful. But of course they ought to be ashamed to offer you such food. Now do you remember that sole? Sole! It was no more sole than this glove's sole. And if it had been cooked a minute, it had been cooked an hour, and waiting. And then look at the prices. Oh yes, I couldn't help seeing the bill.'

'I thought it was awfully cheap,' said he.

'Well, *I* didn't!' said she. 'When you think that a good housekeeper can keep everything going on ten shillings a head a *week*. . . . Why, it's simply scandalous! And I suppose this place is even dearer?'

He avoided the question. 'This is a better place altogether,' he said. 'In fact, I don't know many places in Europe where one can eat better than one does here.'

'Don't you!' she said indulgently, as if saying, 'Well, I know one, at any rate.'

'They say,' he continued, 'that there is no butter used in this place that costs less than three shillings a pound.'

'*No* butter costs them three shillings a pound,' said she.

'Not in London,' said he. 'They have it from Paris.'

'And do you believe that?' she said.

'Yes,' he said.

'Well, I don't. Any one that pays more than one and nine a pound for butter, *at the most*, is a fool, if you'll excuse me saying the word. Not but what this is good butter. I couldn't get as good in Putney for less than eighteen-pence.'

She made him feel like a child who has a great deal to pick up from a kindly but firm sister.

'No, thank you,' she said, a little dryly, to the waiter who had proffered a further supply of chip potatoes.

'Now don't say they're cold,' Priam laughed.

And she laughed also. 'Shall I tell you one thing that put me against these restaurants?' she went on. 'It's the feeling you have that you don't know where the food's *been*. When you've got your kitchen close to your dining-room, you can keep an eye on the stuff from the moment the cart brings it; well, then, you do know a bit where you are. And you can have your dishes served hot. It stands to reason,' she said. 'Where is the kitchen here?'

'Somewhere down below,' he replied apologetically.

'A cellar kitchen!' she exclaimed. 'Why, in Putney they simply can't let houses with cellar kitchens. No! No restaurants and hotels for me – not for *choice* – that is regularly.'

'Still,' he said, with a judicial air, 'hotels are very convenient.'

'Are they?' she said, meaning, 'Prove it.'

'For instance, here, there's a telephone in every room.'

'You don't mean in the bedrooms?'

'Yes, in every bedroom.'

'Well,' she said, 'you wouldn't catch me having a telephone in my bedroom. I should never sleep if I knew there was a telephone in the room! Fancy being forced to telephone every time you want – well! And how is one to know who there is at the other end of the telephone? No, I don't like that. All that's all very well for gentlemen that haven't been used to what I call *com*fort, in a way of speaking. But—'

He saw that if he persisted, nothing soon would be left of that noble pile, the Grand Babylon Hotel, save a heap of ruins. And, further, she genuinely did cause him to feel that throughout his career he had always missed the very best things of life, through being an uncherished, ingenuous, easily satisfied man. A new sensation for him! For if any male in Europe believed in his own capacity to make others make him comfortable, Priam Farll was that male.

'I've never been in Putney,' he ventured, on a new track.

DIFFICULTY OF TRUTH-TELLING

As she informed him, with an ungrudging particularity, about Putney, and her life at Putney, there gradually arose in his brain a vision of a kind of existence such as he had never encountered. Putney had clearly the advantages of a residential town in a magnificent situation. It lay on the slope of a hill whose foot was washed by a glorious stream entitled the Thames, its breast covered with picturesque barges and ornamental rowing boats; an arched bridge spanned this stream, and you went over the bridge in milk-white omnibuses to London. Putney had a street of handsome shops, a purely business street; no one slept there now because of the noise of motors; at eventide the street glittered in its own splendours. There were theatre, music-hall, assembly-rooms, concert-hall, market, brewery, library, and an afternoon tea shop exactly like Regent Street (not that Mrs Challice cared for their alleged China tea); also churches and chapels; and Barnes Common if you walked one way, and Wimbledon Common if you walked another. Mrs Challice lived in Werter Road, Werter Road starting conveniently at the corner of the High Street where the fish-shop was – an establishment where authentic sole was always obtainable, though it was advisable not to buy it on Monday mornings, of course. Putney was a place where you lived unvexed, untroubled. You had your little house, and your furniture, and your ability to look after yourself at all ends, and your knowledge of the prices of everything, and your deep knowledge of human nature, and your experienced forgiveness towards human frailties. You did not keep a servant, because servants were so complicated, and because they could do nothing whatever as well as you could do it yourself. You had a charwoman when you felt idle or when you chose to put the house into the back-yard for an airing. With the charwoman, a pair of gloves for coarser work, and gas stoves, you 'made naught' of domestic labour. You were never worried by ambitions, or by envy, or by the desire to know precisely what the wealthy did and to do likewise. You read when you were not more amusingly occupied, preferring illustrated papers and magazines. You did not traffic with art to any appreciable extent, and you never dreamed of letting it keep you awake at night. You were rich, for the reason that you spent less than you received. You never speculated about the ultimate causes of things, or puzzled yourself concerning the possible developments of society in the next hundred years. When you saw a poor old creature in the street you bought a box of matches off the poor old creature. The social phenomenon which chiefly roused you to just anger was the spectacle of wealthy people making money and so taking the bread out of the mouths of people who needed it. The only apparent blots on existence at Putney were the noise and danger of the High Street, the dearth of reliable laundries, the manners of a middle-aged lady engaged at the post office (Mrs Challice liked the other ladies in the post office), and the absence of a suitable man in the house.

Existence at Putney seemed to Priam Farll to approach the Utopian. It seemed to breathe of romance – the romance of common sense and kindliness and simplicity. It made his own existence to that day appear a futile and unhappy striving after the impossible. Art? What was it? What did it lead to? He was sick of art, and sick of all the forms of activity to which he had hitherto been accustomed and which he had mistaken for life itself.

One little home, fixed and stable, rendered foolish the whole concourse of European hotels.

'I suppose you won't be staying here long?' demanded Mrs Challice.

'Oh no!' he said. 'I shall decide something.'

'Shall you take another place?' she inquired.

'Another place?'

'Yes.' Her smile was excessively persuasive and inviting.

'I don't know,' he said diffidently.

'You must have put a good bit by,' she said, still with the same smile. 'Or perhaps you haven't. Saving's a matter of chance. That's what I always do say. It just depends how you begin. It's a habit. I'd never really blame anybody for not saving. And men—' She seemed to wish to indicate that men were specially to be excused if they did not save.

She had a large mind: that was sure. She understood – things, and human nature in particular. She was not one of those creatures that a man meets with sometimes – creatures who are for ever on the watch to pounce, and who are incapable of making allowances for any male frailty – smooth, smiling creatures, with thin lips, hair a little scanty at the front, with a quietly omniscient 'don't-tell-*me*' tone. Mrs Alice Challice had a mouth as wide as her ideas, and a full under-lip. She was a woman who, as it were, ran out to meet you when you started to cross the dangerous roadway which separates the two sexes. She comprehended because she wanted to comprehend. And when she could not comprehend she would deceive herself that she did: which amounts to the equivalent.

She was a living proof that in her sex social distinctions do not effectively count. Nothing counted, where she was concerned, except a distinction far more profound than any social distinction – the historic distinction between Adam and Eve. She was balm to Priam Farll. She might have been equally balm to King David, Uriah the Hittite, Socrates, Rousseau, Lord Byron, Heine, or Charlie Peace. She would have understood them all. They would all have been ready to cushion themselves on her comfortableness. Was she a lady? Pish! She was a woman.

Her temperament drew Priam Farll like an electrified magnet. To wander about freely in that roomy sympathy of hers seemed to him to be the supreme reward of experience. It seemed like the good inn after the bleak high road, the oasis after the sandstorm, shade after glare, the dressing after the wound, sleep after insomnia, surcease from unspeakable torture. He wanted, in a word, to tell her everything, because she would not demand any difficult explanations. She had given him an opening, in her mention of savings. In reply to her suggestion, 'You must have put a good bit by,' he could casually answer –

'Yes, a hundred and forty thousand pounds.'

And that would lead by natural stages to a complete revealing of the fix in which he was. In five minutes he would have confided in her the principal details, and she would have understood, and then he could describe his agonizing and humiliating half-hour in the Abbey, and she would poor her magic oil on that dreadful abrasion of his sensitiveness. And he would be healed of his hurts, and they would settle between them what he ought to do.

He regarded her as his refuge, as fate's generous compensation to him for the loss of Henry Leek (whose remains now rested in the National Valhalla).

Only, it would be necessary to begin the explanation, so that one thing might by natural stages lead to another. On reflection, it appeared rather abrupt to say –

'Yes, a hundred and forty thousand pounds.'

The sum was too absurdly high (though correct). The mischief was that, unless the sum did strike her as absurdly high, it could not possibly lead by a natural stage to the remainder of the explanation.

He must contrive another path. For instance –

'There's been a mistake about the so-called death of Priam Farll.'

'A mistake?' she would exclaim, all ears and eyes. Then he would say –

'Yes. Priam Farll isn't really dead. It's his valet that's dead.' Whereupon she would burst out –

'But *you* were his valet!'

Whereupon he would simply shake his head, and she would steam forwards –

'Then, who are you?'

Whereupon he would say, as calmly as he could –

'I'm Priam Farll. I'll tell you precisely how it all happened.'

Thus the talk might happen. Thus it would happen, immediately he began. But, as at the Dean's door in Dean's

Yard, so now, he could not begin. He could not utter the necessary words aloud. Spoken aloud, they would sound ridiculous, incredible, insane – and not even Mrs Challice could reasonably be expected to grasp their import, much less believe them.

'*There's been a mistake about the so-called death of Priam Farll.*'

'*Yes, a hundred and forty thousand pounds.*'

No, he could enunciate neither the one sentence nor the other. There are some truths so bizarre that they make you feel self-conscious and guilty before you have begun to state them; you state them apologetically; you blush; you stammer; you have all the air of one who does not expect belief; you look a fool; you feel a fool; and you bring disaster on yourself.

He perceived with the most painful clearness that he could never, never impart to her the terrific secret, the awful truth. Great as she was, the truth was greater, and she would never be able to swallow it.

'What time is it?' she asked suddenly.

'Oh, you mustn't think about time,' he said, with hasty concern.

RESULTS OF RAIN

When the lunch was completely finished and the grill room had so far emptied that it was inhabited by no one except themselves and several waiters who were trying to force them to depart by means of thought transference and uneasy hovering round their table, Priam Farll began to worry his brains in order to find some sane way of spending the afternoon in her society. He wanted to keep her, but he did not know how to keep her. He was quite at a loss. Strange that a man great enough and brilliant enough to get buried in Westminster Abbey had not sufficient of the small change of cleverness to retain the company of a Mrs Alice Challice! Yet so it was. Happily he was buoyed up by the thought that she understood.

'I must be moving off home,' she said, putting her gloves on slowly; and sighed.

'Let me see,' he stammered. 'I think you said Werter Road, Putney?'

'Yes. No. 29.'

'Perhaps you'll let me call on you,' he ventured.

'Oh, do!' she encouraged him.

Nothing could have been more correct, and nothing more banal, than this part of their conversation. He certainly would call. He would travel down to the idyllic Putney to-morrow. He could not lose such a friend, such a balm, such a soft cushion, such a comprehending intelligence. He would bit by bit become intimate with her, and perhaps ultimately he might arrive at the stage of being able to tell her who he was with some chance of being believed. Anyhow, when he did call – and he insisted to himself that it should be extremely soon – he would try another plan with her; he would carefully decide beforehand just what to say and how to say it. This decision reconciled him somewhat to a temporary parting from her.

So he paid the bill, under her sagacious, protesting eyes, and he managed to conceal from those eyes the precise amount of the tip; and then, at the cloak-room, he furtively gave sixpence to a fat and wealthy man who had been watching over his hat and stick. (Highly curious, how those common-sense orbs of hers made all such operations seem excessively silly!) And at last they wandered, in silence, through the corridors and antechambers that led to the courtyard entrance. And through the glass portals Priam Farll had a momentary glimpse of the reflection of light on a cabmen's wet mackintosh. It was raining. It was raining very heavily indeed. All was dry under the glass-roofed colonnades of the courtyard, but the rain rattled like kettledrums on the glass, and the centre of the courtyard was a pond in which a few hansoms were splashing about. Everything – the horses' coats, the cabmen's hats and capes, and the cabmen's red faces – shone and streamed in the torrential summer rain. It is said that geography makes history. In England, and especially in London, weather makes a good deal of history. Impossible to brave that rain, except under the severest pressure of necessity! They were in shelter, and in shelter they must remain.

He was glad, absurdly and splendidly glad.

'It can't last long,' she said, looking up at the black sky, which showed an edge towards the east.

'Suppose we go in again and have some tea?' he said.

Now they had barely concluded coffee. But she did not seem to mind.

'Well,' she said, 'it's always tea-time for *me*.'

He saw a clock. 'It's nearly four,' he said.

Thus justified of the clock, in they went, and sat down in the same seats which they had occupied at the commencement of the adventure in the main lounge. Priam discovered a bell-push, and commanded China tea and muffins. He felt that he now, as it were, had an opportunity of making a fresh start in life. He grew almost gay. He could be gay without sinning against decorum, for Mrs Challice's singular tact had avoided all reference to deaths and funerals.

And in the pause, while he was preparing to be gay, attractive, and in fact his true self, she, calmly stirring China tea, shot a bolt which made him see stars.

'It seems to me,' she observed, 'that we might go farther and fare worse – both of us.'

He genuinely did not catch the significance of it in the first instant, and she saw that he did not.

'Oh,' she proceeded, benevolently and reassuringly, 'I mean it. I'm not gallivanting about. I mean that if you want my opinion I fancy we could make a match of it.'

It was at this point that he saw stars. He also saw a faint and delicious blush on her face, whose complexion was extra-ordinarily fresh and tender.

She sipped China tea, holding each finger wide apart from the others.

He had forgotten the origin of their acquaintance, forgotten that each of them was supposed to have a definite aim in view, forgotten that it was with a purpose that they had exchanged photographs. It had not occurred to him that marriage hung over him like a sword. He perceived the sword now, heavy and sharp, and suspended by a thread of appalling fragility. He dodged. He did not want to lose her, never to see her again; but he dodged.

'I couldn't think—' he began, and stopped.

'Of course it's a very awkward situation for a man,' she went on, toying with muffin. 'I can quite understand how you feel. And with most folks you'd be right. There's very few women that can judge character, and if you started to try and

settle something at once they'd just set you down as a wrong
'un. But I'm not like that. I don't expect any fiddle-faddle.
What I like is plain sense and plain dealing. We both want to
get married, so it would be silly to pretend we didn't,
wouldn't it? And it would be ridiculous of me to look for
courting and a proposal, and all that sort of thing, just as if I'd
never seen a man in his shirt-sleeves. The only question is:
shall we suit each other? I've told you what I think. What do
you think?'

She smiled, honestly, kindly, but piercingly.

What could he say? What would you have said, you being a
man? It is easy, sitting there in your chair, with no Mrs Alice
Challice in front of you, to invent diplomatic replies; but
conceive yourself in Priam's place! Besides, he did think she
would suit him. And most positively he could not bear the
prospect of seeing her pass out of his life. He had been through
that experience once, when his hat blew off in the Tube; and
he did not wish to repeat it.

'Of course you've got no *home*!' she said reflectively, with
such compassion. 'Suppose you come down and just have a
little peep at mine?'

So that evening, a suitably paired couple chanced into the
fishmonger's at the corner of Werter Road, and bought a bit of
sole. At the newspaper shop next door but one placards said:
'Impressive Scenes at Westminster Abbey,' 'Farll funeral,
stately pageant,' 'Great Painter laid to rest,' etc.

CHAPTER VI

A PUTNEY MORNING

Except that there was marrying and giving in marriage, it was
just as though he had died and gone to heaven. Heaven is the
absence of worry and of ambition. Heaven is where you want
nothing you haven't got. Heaven is finality. And this was
finality. On the September morning, after the honeymoon
and the settling down, he arose leisurely, long after his wife,

and, putting on the puce dressing-gown (which Alice much admired), he opened the window wider and surveyed that part of the universe which was comprised in Werter Road and the sky above. A sturdy old woman was coming down the street with a great basket of assorted flowers; he took an immense pleasure in the sight of the old woman; the sight of the old woman thrilled him. Why? Well, there was no reason, except that she was vigorously alive, a part of the magnificent earth. All life gave him joy; all life was beautiful to him. He had his warm bath; the bathroom was not of the latest convenience, but Alice could have made a four-wheeler convenient. As he passed to and fro on the first floor he heard the calm, efficient activities below stairs. She was busy in the mornings; her eyes would seem to say to him, 'Now between my uprising and lunch-time please don't depend on me for intellectual or moral support. I am on the spot, but I am also at the wheel and must not be disturbed.'

Then he descended, fresh as a boy, although the prom-ontory which prevented a direct vision of his toes showed accretions. The front-room was a shrine for his breakfast. She served it herself, in her white apron, promptly on his arrival! Eggs! Toast! Coffee! It was nothing, that breakfast; and yet it was everything. No breakfast could have been better. He had probably eaten about fifteen thousand hotel breakfasts before Alice taught him what a real breakfast was. After serving it she lingered for a moment, and then handed him the 'Daily Telegraph,' which had been lying on a chair.

'Here's your "Telegraph,"' she said cheerfully, tacitly disowning any property or interest in the 'Telegraph.' For her, newspapers were men's toys. She never opened a paper, never wanted to know what was going on in the world. Politics – and all that business of the mere machinery of living: she perfectly ignored it! She lived. She did nothing but live. She lived every hour. Priam felt truly that he had at last got down to the bed-rock of life.

There were twenty pages of the 'Telegraph,' far more matter than a man could read in a day even if he read and read and neither ate nor slept. And all of it so soothing in its rich variety! It gently lulled you; it was the ideal companion for a poached egg; upstanding against the coffee-pot, it stood for the solidity of England in the seas. Priam folded it large; he read all the articles down to the fold; then turned the thing over, and finished all of them. After communing with the 'Telegraph,' he communed with his own secret nature, and wandered about, rolling a cigarette. Ah! The first cigarette! His wanderings led him to the kitchen, or at least as far as the threshold thereof. His wife was at work there. Upon every handle or article that might soil she put soft brown paper, and in addition she often wore house gloves; so that her hands remained immaculate; thus during the earlier hours of the day the house, especially in the region of the fire places, had the air of being in curl papers.

'I'm going out now, Alice,' he said, after he had drawn on his finely polished boots.

'Very well, love,' she replied, pre-occupied with her work. 'Lunch as usual.' She never demanded uxoriousness from him. She had got him. She was sure of him. That satisfied her. Sometimes, like a simple woman who has come into a set of pearls, she would, as it were, take him out of his drawer and look at him, and put him back.

At the gate he hesitated whether to turn to the left, towards High Street, or to the right, towards Oxford Road. He chose the right, but he would have enjoyed himself equally had he chosen the left. The streets through which he passed were populated by domestic servants and tradesmen's boys. He saw white-capped girls cleaning door-knobs or windows, or running along the streets, like escaped nuns, or staring in soft meditation from bedroom windows. And the tradesmen's boys were continually leaping in and out of carts, or off and on tricycles, busily distributing food and drink as though Putney had been a beleaguered city. It was extremely interesting and mysterious – and what made it the more mysterious was that the oligarchy of superior persons for whom these boys and girls so assiduously worked remained invisible. He passed a newspaper shop and found his customary delight in the placards. This morning the 'Daily Illustrated' announced nothing but: 'Portrait of a boy aged 12 who weighs 20 stone.' And the 'Record' whispered in scarlet: 'What the German said to the King. Special.' The 'Journal' cried: 'Surrey's glorious finish.' And the 'Courier' shouted: 'The Unwritten Law in the United States. Another Scandal.'

Not for gold would he have gone behind those placards to
the organs themselves; he preferred to gather from the
placards alone what wonders of yesterday the excellent staid
'Telegraph' had unaccountably missed. But in the 'Financial
Times' he saw: 'Cohoon's Annual Meeting. Stormy Scenes.'
And he bought the 'Financial Times' and put it into his pocket
for his wife, because she had an interest in Cohoon's Brewery,
and he conceived the possibility of her caring to glance at the
report.

THE SIMPLE JOY OF LIFE

After crossing the South-Western Railway, he got into the
Upper Richmond Road, a thoroughfare which always
diverted and amused him. It was such a street of contrasts.
Any one could see that, not many years before, it had been a
sacred street, trod only by feet genteel, and made up of houses
each christened with its own name and each standing in its
own garden. And now energetic persons had put churches
into it, vast red things with gigantic bells, and large drapery
shops, with blouses at six-and-eleven, and court photo-
graphers, and banks, and cigar-stores, and auctioneers' offices.
And all kinds of omnibuses ran along it. And yet somehow it
remained meditative and superior. In every available space
gigantic posters were exhibited. They all had to do with food
or pleasure. There were York hams eight feet high, that a
regiment could not have eaten in a month; shaggy and
ferocious oxen peeping out of monstrous teacups in their
anxiety to be consumed; spouting bottles of ale whose froth
alone would have floated the mail steamers pictured on the
adjoining sheet; and forty different decoctions for imparting
strength. Then after a few score yards of invitation to debauch
there came, with characteristic admirable English common
sense, a cure for indigestion, so large that it would have given
ease to a mastodon who had by inadvertence swallowed an
elephant. And then there were the calls to pleasure.
Astonishing, the quantity of palaces that offered you exactly
the same entertainment twice over on the same night!
Astonishing, the reliance on number in this matter of amuse-

ment! Authenticated statements that a certain performer had
done a certain thing in a certain way a thousand and one times
without interruption were stuck all over the Upper Richmond
Road, apparently in the sure hope that you would rush to see
the thousand and second performance. These performances
were invariably styled original and novel. All the remainder of
free wall space was occupied by philanthropists who were
ready to give away cigarettes at the nominal price of a penny a
packet.

Priam Farll never tired of the phantasmagoria of Upper
Richmond Road. The interminable, intermittent vision of
food dead and alive, and of performers performing the same
performance from everlasting to everlasting, and of millions
and millions of cigarettes ascending from the mouths of
handsome young men in incense to heaven – this rare vision,
of which in all his wanderings he had never seen the like, had
the singular effect of lulling his soul into a profound content.
Not once did he arrive at the end of the vision. No! when he
reached Barnes Station he could see the vision still stretching
on and on; but, filled to the brim, he would get into an
omnibus and return. The omnibus awoke him to other issues:
the omnibus was an antidote. In the omnibus cleanliness was
nigh to godliness. On one pane a soap was extolled, and on
another the exordium, 'For this is a true saying and worthy of
all acceptation,' was followed by the statement of a religious
dogma; while on another pane was an urgent appeal not to do
in the omnibus what you would not do in a drawing-room.
Yes, Priam Farll had seen the world, but he had never seen a
city so incredibly strange, so packed with curious and rare
psychological interest as London. And he regretted that he had
not discovered London earlier in his lifelong search after
romance.

At the corner of the High Street he left the omnibus, and
stopped a moment to chat with his tobacconist. His
tobacconist was a stout man in a white apron, who stood for
ever behind a counter and sold tobacco to the most respected
residents of Putney. All his ideas were connected either with
tobacco or with Putney. A murder in the Strand to that
tobacconist was less than the breakdown of a motor 'bus
opposite Putney Station; and a change of Government less

than a change of programme at the Putney Empire. A rather pessimistic tobacconist, not inclined to believe in a First Cause, until one day a drunken man smashed Salmon and Gluckstein's window down the High Street, whereupon his opinion of Providence went up for several days! Priam enjoyed talking to him, though the tobacconist was utterly impervious to ideas and never gave out ideas. This morning the tobacconist was at his door. At the other corner was the sturdy old woman whom Priam had observed from his window. She sold flowers.

'Fine old woman, that!' said Priam heartily after he and the tobacconist had agreed upon the fact that it was a glorious morning.

'She used to be at the opposite corner by the station until last May but one, when the police shifted her,' said the tobacconist.

'Why did the police shift her?' asked Priam.

'I don't know as I can tell you,' said the tobacconist. 'But I remember her this twelve year.'

'I only noticed her this morning,' said Priam. 'I saw her from my bedroom window, coming down the Werter Road. I said to myself, "She's the finest old woman I ever saw in my life!"'

'Did you now!' murmured the tobacconist. 'She's rare and dirty.'

'I like her to be dirty,' said Priam stoutly. 'She ought to be dirty. She wouldn't be the same if she were clean.'

'I don't hold with dirt,' said the tobacconist calmly. 'She'd be better if she had a bath of a Saturday night like other folks.'

'Well,' said Priam, 'I want an ounce of the usual.'

'Thank *you*, sir,' said the tobacconist, putting down three-halfpence change out of sixpence as Priam thanked him for the packet.

Nothing whatever in such a dialogue! Yet Priam left the shop with a distinct feeling that life was good. And he plunged into the High Street, lost himself in crowds of perambulators and nice womanly women who were bustling honestly about in search of food or raiment. Many of them carried little red books full of long lists of things which they and their admirers and the offspring of mutual affection had eaten or would shortly eat. In the High Street all was luxury: not a necessary in the street. Even the bakers' shops were a mass of sultana and Berlin pancakes. Illuminated calendars, gramophones, corsets, picture postcards, Manilla cigars, bridge-scorers, chocolate, exotic fruit, and commodious mansions – these seemed to be the principal objects offered for sale in High Street. Priam bought a sixpenny edition of Herbert Spencer's 'Essays' for fourpence halfpenny, and passed on to Putney Bridge, whose noble arches divided a first storey of vans and omnibuses from a ground-floor of barges and racing eights. And he gazed at the broad river and its hanging gardens, and dreamed; and was awakened by the roar of an electric train shooting across the stream on a red causeway a few yards below him. And, miles off, he could descry the twin towers of the Crystal Palace, more marvellous than mosques!

'Astounding!' he murmured joyously. He had not a care in the world; and Putney was all that Alice had painted it. In due time, when bells had pealed to right and to left of him, he went home to her.

COLLAPSE OF THE PUTNEY SYSTEM

Now, just at the end of lunch, over the last stage of which they usually sat a long time, Alice got up quickly, in the midst of her Stilton, and, going to the mantelpiece, took a letter therefrom.

'I wish you'd look at that, Henry,' she said, handing him the letter. 'It came this morning, but of course I can't be bothered with that sort of thing in the morning. So I put it aside.'

He accepted the letter, and unfolded it with the professional all-knowing air which even the biggest male fool will quite successfully put on in the presence of a woman if consulted about business. When he had unfolded the thing – it was typed on stiff, expensive, quarto paper – he read it. In the lives of beings like Priam Farll and Alice a letter such as that is a terrible event, unique, earth-arresting; simple recipients are apt, on receiving it, to imagine that the Christian era has come to an end. But tens of thousands of similar letters are sent out from the City every day, and the City thinks nothing of them.

The letter was about Cohoon's Brewery Company, Limited, and it was signed by a firm of solicitors. It referred to the verbatim report, which is said would be found in the financial papers, of the annual meeting of the company held at the Cannon Street Hotel on the previous day, and to the exceedingly unsatisfactory nature of the Chairman's statement. It regretted the absence of Mrs Alice Challice (her change of condition had not yet reached the heart of Cohoon's) from the meeting, and asked her whether she would be prepared to support the action of a committee which had been formed to eject the existing board and which had already a following of 385,000 votes. It finished by asserting that unless the committee was immediately lifted to absolute power the company would be quite ruined.

Priam re-read the letter aloud.

'What does it all mean?' asked Alice quietly.

'Well,' said he, 'that's what it means.'

'Does it mean—?' she began.

'By Jove!' he exclaimed, 'I forgot. I saw something on a placard this morning about Cohoon's, and I thought it might interest you, so I bought it.' So saying, he drew from his pocket the 'Financial Times,' which he had entirely forgotten. There is was: a column and a quarter on the Chairman's speech, and nearly two columns of stormy scenes. The Chairman was the Marquis of Drumgaldy, but his rank had apparently not shielded him from the violence of expletives such as 'Liar!' 'Humbug!' and even 'Rogue!' The Marquis had merely stated, with every formula of apology, that, owing to the extraordinary depreciation in licensed property, the directors had not felt justified in declaring any dividend at all on the Ordinary Shares of the company. He had made this quite simple assertion, and instantly a body of shareholders, less reasonable and more avaricious even than shareholders usually are, had begun to turn the Cannon Street Hotel into a bear garden. One might have imagined that the sole aim of brewery companies was to make money, and that the patriotism of old-world brewers, that patriotism which impelled them to supply an honest English beer to the honest English working-man at a purely nominal price, was scorned and forgotten. One was, indeed, forced to imagine this. In vain the

Marquis pointed out that the shareholders had received a fifteen per cent dividend for years and years past, and that really, for once in a way, they ought to be prepared to sacrifice a temporary advantage for the sake of future prosperity. The thought of those regular high dividends gave rise to no gratitude in shareholding hearts; it seemed merely to render them the more furious. The baser passions had been let loose in the Cannon Street Hotel. The directors had possibly been expecting the baser passions, for a *posse* of policemen was handy at the door, and one shareholder, to save him from having the blood of Marquises on his soul, was ejected. Ultimately, according to the picturesque phrases of the 'Financial Times' report, the meeting broke up in confusion.

'How much have you got in Cohoon's?' Priam asked Alice, after they had looked through the report together.

'All I have is in Cohoon's,' said she, 'except this house. Father left me it like that. He always said there was nothing like a brewery. I've heard him say many and many a time a brewery was better than consols. I think there's 200 £5 shares. Yes, that's it. But of course they're worth much more than that. They're worth about £12 each. All I know is they bring me in £150 a year as regular as the clock. What's that there after "broke up in confusion"?'

She pointed with her finger to a paragraph, and he read in a low voice the fluctuations of Cohoon's Ordinary Shares during the afternoon. They had finished at £6 5s. Mrs Henry Leek had lost over £1,000 in about half a day.

'They've always brought me in £150 a year,' she insisted, as though she had been saying: 'It's always been Christmas Day on the 25th December, and of course it will be the same this year.'

'It doesn't look as if they'd bring you in anything this time,' said he.

'Oh, but Henry!' she protested.

Beer had failed! That was the truth of it. Beer had failed. Who would have guessed that beer could fail in England! The wisest, the most prudent men in Lombard Street had put their trust in beer, as the last grand bulwark of the nation; and even beer had failed. The foundations of England's greatness were, if not gone, going. Insufficient to argue bad management, indiscreet purchases of licences at inflated prices! In the excellent old days a brewery would stand an indefinite amount of bad management! Times were changed. The British workman, caught in a wave of temperance, could no longer be relied upon to drink! It was the crown of his sins against society. Trade unions were nothing to this latest caprice of his, which spread desolation in a thousand genteel homes. Alice wondered what her father would have said, had he lived. On the whole, she was glad that he did not happen to be alive. The shock to him would have been too rude. The floor seemed to be giving way under Alice, melting into a sort of bog that would swallow up her and her husband. For years, without any precise information, but merely by instinct, she had felt that England, beneath the surface, was not quite the island it had been – and here was the awful proof.

She gazed at her husband, as a wife ought to gaze at her husband in a crisis. His thoughts were much vaguer than hers, his thoughts about money being always extremely vague.

'Suppose you went up to the City and saw Mr What's-his-name?' she suggested, meaning the signatory of the letter.

'*Me!*'

It was a cry of the soul aghast, a cry drawn out of him sharply, by a most genuine cruel alarm. Him to go up to the City to interview a solicitor! Why the poor dear woman must be demented! He could not have done it for a million pounds. The thought of it made him sick, raising the whole of his lunch to his throat, as by some sinister magic.

She saw and translated the look on his face. It was a look of horror. And at once she made excuses for him to herself. At once she said to herself that it was no use pretending that her Henry was like other men. He was not. He was a dreamer. He was, at times, amazingly peculiar. But he was her Henry. In any other man than her Henry a hesitation to take charge of his wife's financial affairs would have been ridiculous; it would have been effeminate. But Henry was Henry. She was gradually learning the truth. He was adorable; but he was Henry. With magnificent strength of mind she collected herself.

'No,' she said cheerfully. 'As they're my shares, perhaps I'd better go. Unless we *both* go!' She encountered his eye again, and added quietly: 'No, I'll go alone.'

He sighed his relief. He could not help sighing his relief.

And, after meticulously washing-up and straightening, she departed, and Priam remained solitary with his ideas about married life and the fiscal question.

Alice was assuredly the very mirror of discretion. Never, since that unanswered query as to savings at the Grand Babylon, had she subjected him to any inquisition concerning money. Never had she talked of her own means, save in casual phrase now and then to assure him that there was enough. She had indeed refused bank-notes diffidently offered to her by him, telling him to keep them by him till need of them arose. Never had she discoursed of her own past life, nor led him on to discourse of his. She was one of those women for whom neither the past nor the future seems to exist – they are always so occupied with the important present. He and she had both of them relied on their judgment of character as regarded each other's worthiness and trustworthiness. And he was the last man in the world to be a chancellor of the exchequer. To him, money was a quite uninteresting token that had to pass through your hands. He had always had enough of it. He had always had too much of it. Even at Putney he had had too much of it. The better part of Henry Leek's two hundred pounds had remained in his pockets, and under his own will he had his pound a week, of which he never spent more than a few shillings. His distractions were tobacco (which cost him about twopence a day), walking about and enjoying colour effects and oddities of the streets (which cost him nearly nought), and reading: there were three shops in Putney where all that is greatest in literature could be bought for fourpence halfpenny a volume. Do what he would, he could not read away more than ninepence a week. He was positively accumulating money. You may say that he ought to have compelled Alice to accept money. The idea never occurred to him. In his scheme of things money had not been a matter of sufficient urgency to necessitate an argument with one's wife. She was always welcome to all that he had.

And now suddenly, money acquired urgency in his eyes. It was most disturbing. He was not frightened: he was merely disturbed. If he had ever known the sensation of wanting money and not being able to obtain it, he would probably have been frightened. But this sensation was unfamiliar to him. Not once in his whole career had he hesitated to change gold from fear that the end of gold was at hand.

All kinds of problems crowded round him.

He went out for a stroll to escape the problems. But they accompanied him. He walked through exactly the same streets as had delighted him in the morning. And they had ceased to delight him. This surely could not be ideal Putney that he was in! It must be some other place of the same name. The mismanagement of a brewery a hundred and fifty miles from London; the failure of the British working-man to drink his customary pints in several scattered scores of public-houses, had most unaccountably knocked the bottom out of the Putney system of practical philosophy. Putney posters were now merely disgusting. Putney trade gross and futile, the tobacconist a narrow-minded and stupid bourgeois; and so on.

Alice and he met on their doorstep, each in the act of pulling out a latch-key.

'Oh!' she said, when they were inside, 'it's done for! There's no mistake – it's done for! We shan't get a penny this year, not one penny! And he doesn't think there'll be anything next year either! And the shares'll go down yet, he says. I never heard of such a thing in all my life! Did you?'

He admitted sympathetically that he had not.

After she had been upstairs and come down again her mood suddenly changed.

'Well,' she smiled, 'whether we get anything or not, it's tea-time. So we'll have tea. I've no patience with worrying. I said I should make pastry after tea, and I will, too. See if I don't.'

The tea was, perhaps, slightly more elaborate than usual.

After tea he heard her singing in the kitchen. And he was moved to go and look at her. There she was, with her sleeves turned back, and a large pinafore apron over her rich bosom, kneading flour. He would have liked to approach her and kiss her. But he never could accomplish feats of that kind at unusual moments.

'Oh!' she laughed. 'You can look! *I'm* not worrying. I've no patience with worrying.'

Later in the afternoon he went out; rather like a person who has reasons for leaving inconspicuously. He had made a great, a critical resolve. He passed furtively down Werter Road into the High Street, and then stood a moment outside Stawley's stationery shop, which is also a library, an emporium of leather-bags, and an artists'-colourman's. He entered Stawley's blushing, trembling – he a man of fifty who could not see his own toes – and asked for certain tubes of colour. An energetic young lady who seemed to know all about the graphic arts endeavoured to sell to him a magnificent and complicated box of paints, which opened out into an easel and a stool, and contained a palette of a shape preferred by the late Edwin Long, R.A., a selection of colours which had been approved by the late Lord Leighton, P.R.A., and a patent drying oil which (she said) had been used by Whistler. Priam Farll got away from the shop without this apparatus for the confection of masterpieces, but he did not get away without a sketching-box which he had no intention of buying. The young lady was too energetic for him. He was afraid of being too curt with her lest she should turn on him and tell him that pretence was useless – she knew he was Priam Farll. He felt guilty, and he felt that he looked guilty. As he hurried along the High Street towards the river with the paint-box it appeared to him that policemen observed him inimically and cocked their helmets at him, as who should say: 'See here; this won't do. You're supposed to be in Westminster Abbey. You'll be locked up if you're too brazen.'

The tide was out. He sneaked down to the gravelly shore a little above the steamer pier, and hid himself between the piles, glancing around him in a scared fashion. He might have been about to commit a crime. Then he opened the sketch-box, and oiled the palette, and tried the elasticity of the brushes on his hand. And he made a sketch of the scene before him. He did it very quickly – in less than half an hour. He had made thousands of such colour 'notes' in his life, and he would never part with any of them. He had always hated to part with his notes. Doubtless his Cousin Duncan had them now, if Duncan had discovered his address in Paris, as Duncan probably had.

When it was finished, he inspected the sketch, half shutting his eyes and holding it about three feet off. It was good. Except for a few pencil scrawls done in sheer absentmindedness and hastily destroyed, this was the first sketch he had made since the death of Henry Leek. But it was very good. 'No mistake who's done that!' he murmured; and added: 'That's the devil of it. Any expert would twig it in a minute. There's only one man that could have done it. I shall have to do something worse than that!' He shut up the box, and with a bang, as an amative couple came into sight. He need not have done so, for the couple vanished instantly, in deep disgust at being robbed of their retreat between the piles.

Alice was nearing the completion of pastry when he returned in the dusk; he smelt the delicious proof. Creeping quietly upstairs, he deposited his brushes in an empty attic at the top of the house. Then he washed his hands with especial care, to remove all odour of paint. And at dinner he endeavoured to put on the mien of innocence.

She was cheerful, but it was the cheerfulness of determined effort. They naturally talked of the situation. It appeared that she had a reserve of money in the bank – as much as would suffice her for quite six months. He told her with false buoyancy that there need never be the slightest difficulty as to money; he had money, and he could always earn more.

'If you think that I'm going to let you go into another situation,' she said, 'you're mistaken. That's all.' And her lips were firm.

This staggered him. He never could remember for more than half an hour at a time that he was a retired valet. And it was decidedly not her practice to remind him of the fact. The notion of himself in a situation as valet was half ridiculous and half tragical. He could no more be a valet than he could be a stockbroker or a wire-walker.

'I wasn't thinking of that,' he stammered.

'Then what were you thinking of?' she asked.

'Oh! I don't know!' he said vaguely.

'Because those things they advertise – homework, envelope addressing, or selling gramophones on commission – they're no good, you know!'

He shuddered.

The next morning he bought a 36 by 24 canvas, and more brushes and tubes, and surreptitiously introduced them into the attic. Happily it was the charwoman's day and Alice was busy enough to ignore him. With an old table and the tray out of a travelling-trunk, he arranged a substitute for an easel, and began to try to paint a bad picture from his sketch. But in a quarter of an hour he discovered that he was exactly as fitted to paint a bad picture as to be a valet. He could not sentimentalize the tones, nor falsify the values. He simply could not; the attempt to do so annoyed him. All men are capable of stooping beneath their highest selves, and in several directions Priam Farll could have stooped. But not on canvas! He could only produce his best. He could only render nature as he saw nature. And it was instinct, rather than conscience, that prevented him from stooping.

In three days, during which he kept Alice out of the attic partly by lies and partly by locking the door, the picture was finished; and he had forgotten all about everything except his profession. He had become a different man, a very excited man.

'By Jove,' he exclaimed, surveying the picture, 'I can paint!'

Artists do occasionally soliloquize in this way.

The picture was dazzling! What atmosphere! What poetry! And what profound fidelity to nature's facts! It was precisely such a picture as he was in the habit of selling for £800 or £1,000, before his burial in Westminster Abbey! Indeed, the trouble was that it had 'Priam Farll' written all over it, just as the sketch had!

CHAPTER VII

THE CONFESSION

That evening he was very excited, and he seemed to take no thought to disguise his excitement. The fact was, he could not have disguised it, even if he had tried. The fever of artistic creation was upon him – all the old desires and the old existing joys. His genius had been lying idle, like a lion in a thicket, and now it had sprung forth ravening. For months he had not handled a brush; for months his mind had deliberately avoided

the question of painting, being content with the observation
only of beauty. A week ago, if he had deliberately asked
himself whether he would ever paint again, he might have
answered, 'Perhaps not.' Such is man's ignorance of his own
nature! And now the lion of his genius was standing over him,
its paw on his breast, and making a great noise.

He saw that the last few months had been merely an
interlude, that he would be forced to paint – or go mad; and
that nothing else mattered. He saw also that he could only
paint in one way – Priam Farll's way. If it was discovered that
Priam Farll was not buried in Westminster Abbey; if there was
a scandal, and legal unpleasantness – well, so much the worse!
But he must paint.

Not for money, mind you! Incidentally, of course, he
would earn money. But he had already quite forgotten that life
has its financial aspect.

So in the sitting-room in Werter Road he walked uneasily to
and fro, squeezing between the table and the side-board, and
then skirting the fire-place where Alice sat with a darning
apparatus upon her knees, and her spectacles on – she wore
spectacles when she had to look fixedly at very dark objects.
The room was ugly in a pleasant Putneyish way, with a couple
of engravings after B.W. Leader, R.A., a too realistic wall-
paper, hot brown furniture with ribbed legs, a carpet with the
characteristics of a retired governess who has taken to drink,
and a black cloud on the ceiling over the incandescent burners.
Happily these surroundings did not annoy him. They did not
annoy him because he never saw them. When his eyes were
not resting on beautiful things, they were not in this world of
reality at all. His sole idea about house-furnishing was an easy
chair.

'Harry,' said his wife, 'don't you think you'd better sit
down?'

The calm voice of common sense stopped him in his
circular tour. He glanced at Alice, and she, removing her
spectacles, glanced at him. The seal on his watch-chain
dangled free. He had to talk to some one, and his wife was
there – not only the most convenient but the most proper
person to talk to. A tremendous impulse seized him to tell
her everything; she would understand; she always did under-

stand; and she never allowed herself to be startled. The most singular occurrences, immediately they touched her, were somehow transformed into credible daily, customary events. Thus the disaster of the brewery! She had accepted it as though the ruins of breweries were a spectacle to be witnessed at every street corner.

Yes, he should tell her. Three minutes ago he had no intention of telling her, or any one, anything. He decided in an instant. To tell her his secret would lead up naturally to the picture which he had just finished.'

'I say, Alice,' he said, 'I want to talk to you.'

'Well,' she said, 'I wish you'd talk to me sitting down. I don't know what's come over you this last day or two.'

He sat down. He did not feel really intimate with her at that moment. And their marriage seemed to him, in a way, artificial, scarcely a fact. He did not know that it takes years to accomplish full intimacy between husband and wife.

'You know,' he said, 'Henry Leek isn't my real name.'

Oh, isn't it? she said. 'What does that matter?'

She was not in the least surprised to hear that Henry Leek was not his real name. She was a wise woman, and knew the strangeness of the world. And she had married him simply because he was himself, because he existed in a particular manner (whose charm for her she could not have described) from hour to hour.

'So long as you haven't committed a murder or anything,' she added, with her tranquil smile.

'My real name is Priam Farll,' he said gruffly. The gruffness was caused by timidity.

'I thought Priam Farll was your gentleman's name.'

'To tell you the truth,' he said nervously, 'that was a mistake. That photograph that was sent to you was my photograph.'

'Yes,' she said. 'I know it was. And what of it?'

'I mean,' he blundered on, 'it was my valet that died – not me. You see, the doctor, when he came, thought that Leek was me, and I didn't tell him differently, because I was afraid of all the bother. I just let it slide – and there were other reasons. You know how I am. . . . '

'I don't know what you're talking about,' she said.

'Can't you understand? It's simple enough. I'm Priam Farll, and I had a valet named Henry Leek, and he died, and they thought it was me. Only it wasn't.'

He saw her face change and then compose itself.

'Then it's this Henry Leek that is buried in Westminster Abbey, instead of you?' Her voice was very soft and soothing. And the astonishing woman resumed her spectacles and her long needle.

'Yes, of course.'

Here he burst into the whole story, into the middle of it, continuing to the end, and then going back to the commencement. He left out nothing, and nobody, except Lady Sophia Entwistle.

'I see,' she observed. 'And you've never said a word?'

'Not a word.'

'If I were you I should still keep perfectly silent about it,' she almost whispered persuasively. 'It'll be just as well. If I were you, I shouldn't worry myself. I can quite understand how it happened, and I'm glad you've told me. But don't worry. You've been exciting yourself these last two or three days. I thought it was about my money business, but I see it wasn't. At least that may have brought it on, like. Now the best thing you can do is to forget it.'

She did not believe him! She simply discredited the whole story; and, told in Werter Road, like that, the story did sound fantastic; it did come very near to passing belief. She had always noticed a certain queerness in her husband. His sudden gaieties about a tint in the sky or the gesture of a horse in the street, for example, were most uncanny. And he had peculiar absences of mind that she could never account for. She was sure that he must have been a very bad valet. However, she did not marry him for a valet, but for a husband; and she was satisfied with her bargain. What if he did suffer under a delusion? The exposure of that delusion merely crystallized into a definite shape her vague suspicions concerning his mentality. Besides, it was a harmless delusion. And it explained things. It explained among other things, why he had gone to stay at the Grand Babylon Hotel. That must have been the inception of the delusion. She was glad to know the worst.

She adored him more than ever.

There was a silence.

'No,' she repeated, in the most matter-of-fact tone, 'I should say nothing, in your place. I should forget it.'

'You would?' he drummed on the table.

'I should! And whatever you do, don't worry.' Her accents were the coaxing accents of a nurse with a child – or with a lunatic.

He perceived now with the utmost clearness that she did not believe a word of what he had said, and that in her magnificent and calm sagacity she was only trying to humour him. He had expected to disturb her soul to its profoundest depths; he had expected that they would sit up half the night discussing the situation. And lo! – 'I should forget it,' indulgently! And a mild continuance of darning!

He had to think, and think hard.

TEARS

'Henry,' she called out the next morning, as he disappeared up the stairs. 'What *are* you doing up there?'

She had behaved exactly as if nothing had happened; and she was one of those women whose prudent policy it is to let their men alone even to the furthest limit of patience; but she had nerves, too, and they were being affected. For three days Henry had really been mysterious!

He stopped, and put his head over the banisters, and in a queer, moved voice answered –

'Come and see.'

Sooner or later she must see. Sooner or later the already distended situation must get more and more distended until it burst with a loud report. Let the moment be sooner, he swiftly decided.

So she went and saw.

Half-way up the attic stairs she began to sniff, and as he turned the knob of the attic door for her she said 'What a smell of paint! I fancied yesterday—'

If she had been clever enough, she would have said, 'What a smell of masterpieces!' But her cleverness lay in other fields.

'You surely haven't been aspinalling that bath-room chair?
. . . Oh!'

This loud exclamation escaped from her as she entered the
attic and saw the back of the picture which Priam had lodged
on the said bath-room chair – filched by him from the
bath-room on the previous day. She stepped to the vicinity of
the window and obtained a good view of the picture. It was
brilliantly shining in the light of morn. It looked glorious; it
was a fit companion of many pictures from the same hand
distributed among European galleries. It had that priceless
quality, at once noble and radiant, which distinguished all
Priam's work. It transformed the attic; and thousands of
amateurs and students, from St Petersburg to San Francisco,
would have gone into that attic with their hats off and a thrill
in the spine, had they known what was there and had they
been invited to enter and worship. Priam himself was pleased;
he was delighted; he was enthusiastic. And he stood near the
picture, glancing at it and then glancing at Alice, nervously
like a mother whose sister-in-law has come to look at the
baby. As for Alice, she said nothing. She had first of all to take
in the fact that her husband had been ungenerous enough to
keep her quite in the dark as to the nature of his secret
activities; then she had to take in the fact of the picture.

'Did you do that?' she said limply.

'Yes,' said he, with all the casualness that he could assume.
'How does it strike you?' And to himself: 'This'll make her see
I'm not a mere lunatic. This'll give her a shaking up.'

'I'm sure it's beautiful,' she said kindly, but without the
slightest conviction. 'What is it? Is that Putney Bridge?'

'Yes,' he said.

'I thought it was. I thought it must be. Well, I never knew you
could paint. It's beautiful – for an amateur.' She said this firmly
and yet endearingly and met his eyes with her eyes. It was her
tactful method of politely causing him to see that she had not
accepted last night's yarn very seriously. His eyes fell, not hers.

'No, no, no!' he expostulated with quick vivacity, as she
stepped towards the canvas. 'Don't come any nearer. You're
at just the right distance.'

'Oh! If you don't *want* me to see it close,' she humoured
him. 'What a pity you haven't put an omnibus on the bridge!'

'There is one,' said he. '*That's* one.' He pointed.

'Oh yes! Yes, I see. But, you know, I think it looks rather more like a Carter Paterson van than an omnibus. If you could paint some letters on it – 'Union Jack' or 'Vanguard', then people would be sure. But it's beautiful. I suppose you learnt to paint from your—' She checked herself, 'What's that red streak behind?'

'That's the railway bridge,' he muttered.

'Oh, of course it is! How silly of me! Now, if you were to put a train on that. The worst of trains in pictures is that they never seem to be going along. I've noticed that on the sides of furniture vans, haven't you? But if you put a signal, against it, then people would understand that the train had stopped, I'm not sure whether there *is* a signal on the bridge, though.'

He made no remark.

'And I see that's the Elk public-house there on the right. You've just managed to get it in. I can recognize that quite easily. Any one would.'

He still made no remark.

'What are you going to do with it?' she asked gently.

'Going to sell it, my dear,' he replied grimly. 'It may surprise you to know that that canvas is worth at the very least £800. There would be a devil of a row and a rumpus in Bond Street and elsewhere if they knew I was painting here instead of rotting in Westminster Abbey. I don't propose to sign it – I seldom did sign my pictures – and we shall see what we shall see . . . I've got fifteen hundred for little things not so good as that. I'll let it go for what it'll fetch. We shall soon be wanting money.'

The tears rose to Alice's eyes. She saw that he was infinitely more mad than she imagined – with his £800 and his £1,500 for daubs of pictures that conveyed no meaning whatever to the eye! Why, you could purchase real, professional pictures, of lakes and mountains, exquisitely finished, at the frame-makers in High Street for three pounds apiece! And here he was rambling in hundreds and thousands! She saw that that extraordinary notion about being able to paint was a natural consequence of the pathetic delusion to which he had given utterance yesterday. And she wondered what would follow next. Who could have guessed that the seeds of lunacy were in

such a man? Yes, harmless lunacy, but lunacy nevertheless!
She distinctly remembered the little shock with which she had
learned that he was staying at the Grand Babylon on his own
account, as a wealthy visitor. She thought it bizarre, but she
certainly had not taken it for a sign of lunacy. And yet it had
been a sign of madness. And the worst of harmless lunacy was
that it might develop at any moment into harmful lunacy.

There was one thing to do, and only one: keep him quiet,
shield him from all troubles and alarms. It was disturbance of
spirit which induced these mental derangements. His master's
death had upset him. And now he had been upset by her
disgraceful brewery company.

She made a step towards him, and then hesitated. She had to
form a plan of campaign all in a moment! She had to keep her
wits and to use them! How could she give him confidence
about his absurd picture? She noticed that naïve look that
sometimes came into his eyes, a boyish expression that gave
the lie to his greying beard and his generous proportions.

He laughed, until, as she came closer, he saw the tears on
her eyelids. Then he ceased laughing. She fingered the edge of
his coat cajolingly.

'It's a beautiful picture!' she repeated again and again. 'And
if you like I will see if I can sell it for you. But, Henry—'

'Well?'

'Please, please don't bother about money. We shall have
heaps. There's no occasion for you to bother, and I won't *have*
you bothering.'

'What are you crying for?' he asked in a murmur.

'It's only – only because I think it's so nice of you trying to
earn money like that,' she lied. 'I'm not really crying.'

And she ran away, downstairs, really crying. It was excessively
comic, but he had better not follow her, lest he might cry too. . . .

A PATRON OF THE ARTS

A lull followed this crisis in the affairs of No. 29 Werter Road.
Priam went on painting, and there was now no need for
secrecy about it. But his painting was not made a subject of
conversation. Both of them hesitated to touch it, she from

tact, and he because her views on the art seemed to him to be
lacking in subtlety. In every marriage there is a topic – there
are usually several – which the husband will never broach to
the wife, out of respect for his respect for her. Priam scarcely
guessed that Alice imagined him to be on the way to lunacy.
He thought she merely thought him queer as artists *are* queer
to non-artists. And he was accustomed to that; 'Henry Leek
had always thought him queer. As for Alice's incredulous
attitude towards the revelation of his identity, he did not
mentally accuse her of treating him as either a liar or a
madman. On reflection he persuaded himself that she regarded
the story as a bad joke, as one of his impulsive, capricious
essays in the absurd.

Thus the march of evolution was apparently arrested in
Werter Road during three whole days. And then a singular
event happened, and progress was resumed. Priam had been
out since early morning on the river-side, sketching, and had
reached Barnes, from which town he returned over Barnes
Common, and so by the Upper Richmond Road to High
Street. He was on the south side of Upper Richmond Road,
whereas his tobacconist's shop was on the north side, near the
corner. An unfamiliar peculiarity of the shop caused him to
cross the street, for he was not in want of tobacco. It was the
look of the window that drew him. He stopped on the refuge
in the centre of the street. There was no necessity to go
farther. His picture of Putney Bridge was in the middle of the
window. He stared at it fixedly. He believed his eyes, for his
eyes were the finest part of him and never deceived him; but
perhaps if he had been a person with ordinary eyes he would
scarce have been able to believe them. The canvas was
indubitably there present in the window. It had been put in a
cheap frame such as is used for chromographic advertisements
of ships, soups, and tobacco. He was almost sure that he had
seen that same frame, within the shop round a pictorial
announcement of Taddy's Snuff. The tobacconist had probably removed the eighteenth-century aristocrat with this
fingers to his nose from the frame, and replaced him with
Putney Bridge. In any event the frame was about half an inch
too long for the canvas, but the gap was scarcely observable.
On the frame was a large notice, 'For sale.' And around it

were the cigars of two hemispheres, from Syak Whiffs at a
penny each to precious Murias; and cigarettes of every
allurement; and the multitudinous fragments of all advertised
tobaccos; and meerschaums and briars, and patent pipes and
diagrams of their secret machinery; and cigarette and cigar
holders laid on plush; and pocket receptacles in aluminium and
other precious metals.

Shining there, the picture had a most incongruous
appearance. He blushed as he stood on the refuge. It seemed to
him that the mere incongruity of the spectacle must inevitably
attract crowds, gradually blocking the street, and that when
some individual not absolutely a fool in art had perceived the
quality of the picture – well, then the trouble of public
curiosity and of journalistic inquisitiveness would begin. He
wondered that he could ever have dreamed of concealing his
identity on canvas. The thing simply shouted 'Priam Farll,'
every inch of it. In any exhibition of pictures in London, Paris,
Rome, Milan, Munich, New York, or Boston it would have
been the cynosure, the target of ecstatic admirations. It was
just another work as his celebrated 'Pont d'Austerlitz,' which
hung in the Luxembourg. And neither a frame of 'chemical
gold' nor the extremely variegated coloration of the other
merchandise on sale could kill it.

However, there were no signs of a crowd. People passed to
and fro, just as though there had not been a masterpiece within
ten thousands miles of them. Once a servant girl, a loaf of
bread in her arms, stopped to glance at the window, but in an
instant she was gone, running.

Priam's first instinctive movement had been to plunge into
the shop, and demand from his tobacconist an explanation of
the phenomenon. But of course, he checked himself. Of
course he knew that the presence of his picture in the window
could only be due to the enterprise of Alice.

He went slowly home.

The sound of his latchkey in the keyhole brought her into
the hall ere he had opened the door.

'Oh, Henry,' she said – she was quite excited – 'I must tell
you. I was passing Mr Aylmer's this morning just as he was
dressing his window, and the thought struck me that he might
put your picture in. So I ran in and asked him. He said he

would if he could have it at once. So I came and got it. He found a frame, and wrote out a ticket, and asked after you. No one could have been kinder. You must go and have a look at it. I shouldn't be at all surprised if its gets sold like that.'

Priam answered nothing for a moment. He could not.

'What did Aylmer say about it?' he asked.

'Oh!' said his wife quickly, 'you can't expect Mr Aylmer to understand these things. It's not in his line. But he was glad to oblige us. I saw that he arranged it nicely.'

'Well,' said Priam discreetly, 'that's all right. Supposing we had lunch?'

Curious – her relations with Mr Aylmer! It was she who had recommended him to go to Mr Aylmer's when, on the first morning of his residence in Putney, he had demanded, 'Any decent tobacconist in this happy region?'

He had suspected that, had it not been for Aylmer's bedridden and incurable wife, Alice's name might have been Aylmer. He suspected Aylmer of a hopeless passion for Alice. He was glad that Alice had not been thrown away on Aylmer. He could not imagine himself now without Alice. In spite of her ideas on the graphic arts, Alice was his air, his atmosphere, his oxygen; and also his umbrella to shield him from the hail of untoward circumstances. Curious – the process of love! It was the power of love that had put the picture in the tobacconist's window.

Whatever power had put it there, no power seemed strong enough to get it out again. It lay exposed in the window for weeks and weeks and never drew a crowd, nor caused a sensation of any kind! Not a word in the newspapers! London, the acknowledged art-centre of the world, calmly went its way. The sole immediate result was that Priam changed his tobacconist, and the direction of his promenades.

At last another singular event happened.

Alice beamingly put five sovereigns into Priam's hand one evening.

'It's been sold for five guineas,' she said, joyous. 'Mr Aylmer didn't want to keep anything for himself, but I insisted on his having the odd shillings. I think it's splendid, simply splendid! Of course I always *did* think it was a beautiful picture,' she added.

The fact was that this astounding sale for so large a sum as five pounds, of a picture done in the attic by her Henry, had enlarged her ideas of Henry's skill. She could no longer regard his painting as the caprice of a gentle lunatic. There was something *in* it. And now she wanted to persuade herself that she had known from the first there was something in it.

The picture had been bought by the eccentric and notorious landlord of the Elk Hotel, down by the river, on a Sunday afternoon, when he was – not drunk, but more optimistic than the state of English society warrants. He liked the picture because his public-house was so unmistakably plain in it. He ordered a massive gold frame for it, and hung it in his saloon-bar. His career as a patron of the arts was unfortunately cut short by an order signed by his doctors for his incarceration in a lunatic asylum. All Putney had been saying for years that he would end in the asylum, and all Putney was right.

CHAPTER VIII

AN INVASION

One afternoon, in December, Priam and Alice were in the sitting-room together, and Alice was about to prepare tea. The drawn-thread cloth was laid diagonally on the table (because Alice had seen cloths so laid on model tea-tables in model rooms at Waring's), the strawberry jam occupied the northern point of the compass, and the marmalade was antarctic, while brittle cakes and spongy cakes represented the occident and the orient respectively. Bread and butter stood, rightly, for the centre of the universe. Silver ornamented the spread, and Alice's two teapots (for she would never allow even Chinese tea to remain on the leaves for more than five minutes) and Alice's water-jug with the patent balanced lid, occupied a tray off the cloth. At some distance, but still on the table, a kettle moaned over a spirit lamp. Alice was cutting bread for toast. The fire was of the right redness for toast, and a toasting-fork lay handy. As winter advanced, Alice's teas had a tendency to become cosier and cosier, and also more luxurious, more of a ritualistic ceremony. And to avoid the trouble and danger of going through a cold passage to the kitchen, she arranged matters so that the entire operation could be performed with comfort and decency in the sitting-room itself.

Priam was rolling cigarettes, many of them, and placing them, as he rolled them, in order on the mantelpiece. A happy, mild couple! And a couple, one would judge from the richness of the tea, with no immediate need of money. Over two years, however, had passed since the catastrophe to Cohoon's, and Cohoon's had in no way recovered therefrom. Yet money had been regularly found for the household. The manner of its finding was soon to assume importance in the careers of Priam and Alice. But, ere that moment, an astonishing and vivid experience happened to them. One might have supposed that, in the life of Priam Farll at least, enough of the astonishing and the vivid had already happened. Nevertheless, what had already happened was as customary and exciting as addressing envelopes, compared to the next event.

The next event began at the instant when Alice was sticking the long fork into a round of bread. There was a knock at the front door, a knock formidable and reverberating, a knock of fate, perhaps, but fate disguised as a coal-heaver.

Alice answered it. She always answered knocks; Priam never. She shielded him from every rough or unexpected contact, just as his valet used to do. The gas in the hall was not lighted, and so she stopped to light it, darkness having fallen. Then she opened the door, and saw in the gloom, a short, thin woman standing on the step, a woman of advanced middle-age, dressed with a kind of shabby neatness. It seemed impossible that so frail and unimportant a creature could have made such a noise on the door.

'Is this Mr Henry Leek's?' asked the visitor, in a dissatisfied, rather weary tone.

'Yes,' said Alice. Which was not quite true. 'This' was assuredly hers, rather than her husband's.

'Oh!' said the woman, glancing behind her; and entered nervously, without invitation.

At the same moment three male figures sprang, or rushed, out of the strip of front garden, and followed the woman into the hall, lunging up against Alice, and breathing loudly. One of the trio was a strong, heavy-faced, heavy–handed, louring young man of some thirty years (it seemed probable that he was the knocker), and the others were curates, with the proper physical attributes of curates; that is to say, they were of ascetic habit and clean-shaven and had ingenuous eyes.

The hall now appeared like the antechamber of a May meeting, and as Alice had never seen it so peopled before, she vented a natural exclamation of surprise.

'Yes,' said one of the curates fiercely. 'You may say "Lord," but we were determined to get in, and in we have got. John, shut the door. Mother, don't put yourself about.'

John, being the heavy-faced and heavy-handed man, shut the door.

'Where is Mr Henry Leek?' demanded the other curate.

Now Priam, whose curiosity had been excusably excited by the unusual sounds in the hall, was peeping through a chink of the sitting-room door, and the elderly woman caught the glint of his eyes. She pushed open the door, and, after a few seconds' inspection of him, said–

'There you are, Henry! After thirty years! To think of it!'

Priam was utterly at a loss.

'I'm his wife, ma'am,' the visitor continued sadly to Alice. 'I'm sorry to have to tell you. I'm his wife. I'm the rightful Mrs Henry Leek, and these are my sons, come with me to see that I get justice.'

Alice recovered very quickly from the shock of amazement. She was a woman not easily to be startled by the vagaries of human nature. She had often heard of bigamy, and that her husband should prove to be a bigamist did not throw her into a swoon. She at once, in her own mind, began to make excuses for him. She said to herself, as she inspected the real Mrs Henry Leek, that the real Mrs Henry Leek had certainly the temperament which manufactures bigamists. She understood how a person may slide into bigamy. And after thirty years! . . . She never thought of bigamy as a crime, nor did it occur to her to run out and drown herself for shame because she was not properly married to Priam!

No, it has to be said in favour of Alice that she invariably took things as they were.

'I think you'd better all come in and sit down quietly,' she said.

'Eh! It's very kind of you,' said the mother of the curates limply.

The last thing that the curates wanted to do was to sit down quietly. But they had to sit down. Alice made them sit side by side on the sofa. The heavy, elder brother, who had not spoken a word, sat on a chair between the sideboard and the door. Their mother sat on a chair near the table. Priam fell into his easy chair between the fireplace and the sideboard. As for Alice, she remained standing; she showed no nervousness except in her handling of the toasting-fork.

It was a great situation. But unfortunately ordinary people are so unaccustomed to the great situation, that, when it chances to come, they feel themselves incapable of living up to it. A person gazing in at the window, and unacquainted with the facts, might have guessed that the affair was simply a tea-party at which the guests had arrived a little too soon, and where no one was startlingly proficient in the art of small-talk.

Still, the curates were apparently bent on doing their best.

'Now, mother!' one of them urged her.

The mother, as if a spring had been touched in her, began: 'He married me just thirty years ago, ma'am; and four months after my eldest was born – that's John there' (pointing to the corner near the door) – 'he just walked out of the house and left me. I'm sorry to have to say it. Yes, sorry I am! But there it is. And never a word had I ever given him! And eight months after that my twins were born. That's Harry and Matthew' – (pointing to the sofa) – 'Harry I called after his father because I thought he was like him, and just to show I bore no ill-feeling, and hoping he'd come back! And there I was with these three little children! And not a word of explanation did I ever have. I heard of Harry five years later – when Johnnie was nearly five – but he was on the Continent and I couldn't go trapesing about with three babies. Besides, if I *had* gone! . . . Sorry I am to say it, ma'am; but many's the time he's beaten me, yes, with his hands and his fists! He's knocked me about a bit. And I never gave him a word back.

He was my husband, for better for worse, and I forgave him and
I still do. Forgive and forget, that's what I say. We only heard of
him through Matthew being second curate at St Paul's, and in
charge of the Mission Hall. It was your milkman that happened
to tell Matthew that he had a customer same name as himself.
And you know how one thing leads to another. So we're here!'

'I never saw this lady in my life,' said Priam excitedly, 'and
I'm absolutely certain I never married her. I never married any
one, except, of course, you, Alice!'

'Then how do you explain this, sir?' exclaimed Matthew, the
younger twin, jumping up and taking a blue paper from his
pocket. 'Be so good as to pass this to father,' he said, handing the
paper to Alice.

Alice inspected the document. It was a certificate of the
marriage of Henry Leek, valet, and Sarah Featherstone,
spinster, at a registry office in Paddington. Priam also inspected
it. This was one of Leek's escapades! No revelations as to the
past of Henry Leek would have surprised him. There was
nothing to be done except to give a truthful denial of identity
and to persist in that denial. Useless to say soothingly to the lady
visitor that she was the widow of a gentleman who had been laid
to rest in Westminster Abbey!

'I know nothing about it,' said Priam doggedly.

'I suppose you'll deny, sir, that your name is Henry Leek,'
said Henry, jumping up to stand by Matthew.

'I deny everything,' said Priam doggedly. How could he
explain? If he had not been able to convince Alice that he was not
Henry Leek, could he hope to convince these visitors?

'I suppose, madam,' Henry continued, addressing Alice in
impressive tones as if she were a crowded congregation, 'that at
any rate you and my father are – er – living here together under
the name of Mr and Mrs Henry Leek!'

Alice merely lifted her eyebrows.

'It's all a mistake,' said Priam impatiently. Then he had a
brilliant inspiration. 'As if there was only one Henry Leek in the
world!'

'Do you really recognize my husband?' Alice asked.

'Your husband, madam!' Matthew protested, shocked.

'I wouldn't say that I recognize him as he *was*,' said the real
Mrs Henry Leek. 'No more than he recognizes me. After thirty

years! . . . Last time I saw him he was only twenty-two or twenty-three. But he's the same sort of man, and he has the same eyes. And look at Henry's eyes. Besides, I heard twenty-five years ago that he'd gone into service with a Mr Priam Farll, a painter or something, him that was buried in Westminster Abbey. And everybody in Putney knows that this gentleman—'

'Gentleman!' murmured Matthew, discontented.

'Was valet to Mr Priam Farll. We've heard that everywhere.'

'I suppose you'll not deny,' said Henry the younger, 'that Priam Farll wouldn't be likely to have *two* valets named Henry Leek?'

Crushed by this Socratic reasoning, Priam kept silent, nursing his knees and staring into the fire.

Alice went to the sideboard where she kept her best china, and took out three extra cups and saucers.

'I think we'd all better have some tea,' she said tranquilly. And then she got the tea-caddy and put seven teaspoonfuls of tea into one of the tea pots.

'It's very kind of you, I'm sure,' whimpered the authentic Mrs Henry Leek.

'Now, mother, don't give way!' the curate admonished her.

'Don't you remember, Henry,' she went on whimpering to Priam, 'how you said you wouldn't be married in a church, not for anybody! And how I gave way to you, like I always did? And don't you remember how you wouldn't let poor little Johnnie be baptized? Well, I do hope your opinions have altered. Eh, but it's strange, it's strange, how two of your sons, and just them two that you'd never set eyes on until this day, should have made up their minds to go into the Church. And thanks to Johnnie, there, they've been able to. If I was to tell you all the struggles we've had, you wouldn't believe me. They were clerks, and they might have been clerks to this day, if it hadn't been for Johnnie. But Johnnie could always earn money. It's that engineering! And now Matthew's second curate at St Paul's and getting fifty pounds a year, and Henry'll have a curacy next month at Bermondsey – it's been promised, and all thanks to Johnnie!' She wept.

Johnnie, in the corner, who had so far done nought but knock on the door, maintained stiffly his policy of non-interference.

Priam Farll, angry, resentful, and quite untouched by the recital, shrugged his shoulders. He was animated by the sole desire to fly from the widow and progeny of his late valet. But he could not fly. The Herculean John was too close to the door. So he shrugged his shoulders a second time.

'Yes, sir,' said Matthew, 'you may shrug your shoulders, but you can't shrug us out of existence. Here we are, and you can't get over us. You are our father, and I presume that a kind of respect is due to you. Yet how can you hope for our respect? Have you earned it? Did you earn it when you ill-treated our poor mother? Did you earn it when you left her, with the most inhuman cruelty, to fend for herself in the world? Did you earn it when you abandoned your children born and unborn? You are a bigamist, sir; a deceiver of woman! Heaven knows—'

'Would you mind just toasting this bread?' Alice interrupted his impassioned discourse by putting the loaded toasting-fork into his hand, 'while I make the tea?'

It was a novel way of stopping a mustang in full career, but it succeeded.

While somewhat perfunctorily holding the fork to the fire Matthew glared about him, to signify his righteous horror, and other sentiments.

'Please don't burn it,' said Alice gently. 'Suppose you were to sit down on this footstool.' And then she poured boiling water on the tea, put the lid on the pot, and looked at the clock to note the exact second at which the process of infusion had begun.

'Of course,' burst out Henry, the twin of Matthew, 'I need not say, madam, that you have all our sympathies. You are in a—'

'Do you mean me?' Alice asked.

In an undertone Priam could be heard obstinately repeating, 'Never set eyes upon her before! Never set eyes on the woman before!'

'I do, madam,' said Henry, not to be cowed nor deflected from his course. 'I speak for all of us. You have our sympathies. You could not know the character of the man you married, or rather with whom you went through the cere-mony of marriage. However, we have heard, by inquiry, that you made his acquaintance through the medium of a matrimonial agency; and indirectly, when one does that sort of thing, one takes one's chance. Your position is an extremely delicate one; but it is not too much to say that you brought it on yourself. In my work, I have encountered many sad instances of the result of lax moral principles; but I little thought to encounter the saddest of all in my own family. The discovery is just as great a blow to us as it is to you. We have suffered; my mother has suffered. And now, I fear, it is your turn to suffer. You are not this man's wife. Nothing can make you his wife. Yet you are living in the same house with him – under circumstances – er – without a chaperon. I hesitate to characterize your situation in plain words. It would scarcely become me, or mine, to do so. But really no lady could possibly find herself in a situation more false than – I am afraid there is only one word, open immorality, and – er – to put yourself right with society there is one thing, and only one, left for you to – er – do. I – I speak for the family, and I—'

'Sugar?' Alice questioned the mother of curates.

'Yes, please.'

'One lump, or two?'

'Two, please.'

'Speaking for the family—' Henry resumed.

'Will you kindly pass this cup to your mother?' Alice suggested.

Henry was obliged to take the cup. Excited by the fever of eloquence, he unfortunately upset it before it had reached his mother's hands.

'Oh, Henry!' murmured the lady, mournfully aghast. 'You always were so clumsy! And a clean cloth, too!'

'Don't mention it, please,' said Alice, and then to *her* Henry: 'My dear, just run into the kitchen, and bring me something to wipe this up. Hanging behind the door – you'll see.'

Priam sprang forward with astonishing celerity. And the occasion brooking no delay, the guardian of the portal could not but let him pass. In another moment the front door banged. Priam did not return. And Alice staunched the flow of tea with a clean, stiff serviette taken from the sideboard drawer.

A DEPARTURE

The family of the late Henry Leek, each with a cup in hand,
experienced a certain difficulty in maintaining the interview at
the pitch set by Matthew and Henry. Mrs Leek, their mother,
frankly gave way to soft tears while eating bread and butter,
jam and zebra-like toast. John took everything that Alice
offered to him in gloomy and awkward silence.

'Does he mean to come back?' Matthew demanded at
length. He had risen from the footstool

'Who?' asked Alice.

Matthew paused, and then said, savagely and deliberately:
'Father.'

Alice smiled. 'I'm afraid not. I'm afraid he's gone out. You
see, he's a rather peculiar man. It's not the slightest use me
trying to drive him. He can only be led. He has his good
points – I can speak candidly as he isn't here, and I *will* – he has
his good points. When Mrs Leek, as I suppose she calls herself,
spoke about his cruelty to her – well, I understood that. Far be
it from me to say a word against him; he's often very good to
me, but – another cup, Mr John?'

John advanced to the table without a word, holding his cup.

'You don't mean to say, ma'am,' said Mrs Leek, 'that he—?'

Alice nodded grievously.

Mrs Leek burst into tears. 'When Johnnie was barely five
weeks old,' she said, 'he would twist my arm. And he kept me
without money. And once he locked me up in the cellar. And
one morning when I was ironing he snatched the hot iron out
of my hand and—'

'Don't! Don't!' Alice soothed her. 'I know. I know all you
can tell me. I know because I've been through—'

'You don't mean to say he threatened *you* with the flat-
iron?'

'If threatening was only all!' said Alice, like a martyr.

'Then he's not changed in all these years!' wept the mother
of curates.

'If he has, it's for the worse,' said Alice. 'How was I to tell?'
she faced the curates. 'How could I know? And yet nobody,
nobody, could be nicer than he is at times!'

'That's true, that's true,' responded the authentic Mrs
Henry Leek. 'He was always so changeable, so queer.'

'Queer!' Alice took up the word. 'That's it. Queer! I don't
think he's *quite* right in his head, not quite right. He has the
very strangest fancies. I never take any notice of them, but
they're there. I seldom get up in the morning without
thinking. "Well, perhaps to-day he'll have to be taken off."'

'Taken off?'

'Yes, to Hanwell, or wherever it is. And you must remember,' she said, gazing firmly at the curates, 'you've got his
blood in your veins. Don't forget that. I suppose you want to
make him go back to you, Mrs Leek, as he certainly ought.'

'Ye-es,' murmured Mrs Leek feebly.

'Well, if you can persuade him to go,' said Alice, 'if you can
make him see his duty, you're welcome. But I'm sorry for
you. I think I ought to tell you that this is my house, and my
furniture. He's got nothing at all. I expect he never could save.
Many's the blow he's laid on me in anger, but all the same I
pity him. I pity him. And I wouldn't like to leave him in the
lurch. Perhaps these three strong young men'll be able to do
something with him. But I'm not sure. He's very strong. And
he has a way of leaping out so sudden like.'

Mrs Leek shook her head as memories of the past rose up in
her mind.

'The fact is,' said Matthew sternly, 'he ought to be prose-
cuted for bigamy. That's what ought to be done.'

'Most decidedly,' Henry concurred.

'You're quite right! You're quite right!' said Alice. 'That's
only justice. Of course he'd deny that he was the same Henry
Leek. He'd deny it like anything. But in the end I dare say
you'd be able to prove it. The worst of these law cases is
they're so expensive. It means private detectives and all sorts
of things, I believe. Of course there'd be the scandal. But don't
mind me! I'm innocent. Everybody knows me in Putney, and
has done this twenty years. I don't know how it would suit
you, Mr Henry and Mr Matthew, as clergymen, to have your
own father in prison. That's as may be. But justice is justice,
and there's too many men going about deceiving simple,
trusting women. I've often heard such tales. Now I know
they're all true. It's a mercy my own poor mother hasn't lived

to see where I am to-day. As for my father, old as he was, if he'd been alive, there'd have been horse-whipping, that I do know.'

After some rather pointless and disjointed remarks from the curates, a sound came from the corner near the door. It was John's cough.

'Better clear out of this!' John ejaculated. Such was his first and last oral contribution to the scene.

IN THE BATH

Priam Farll was wandering about the uncharted groves of Wimbledon Common, and uttering soliloquies in language that lacked delicacy. He had rushed forth, in his haste, without an overcoat, and the weather was blusterously inclement. But he did not feel the cold; he only felt the keen wind of circumstance.

Soon after the purchase of his picture by the lunatic landlord of a fully licensed house, he had discovered that the frame-maker in High Street knew a man who would not be indisposed to buy such pictures as he could paint, and transactions between him and the frame-maker had developed into a regular trade. The usual price paid for canvases was ten pounds, in cash. By this means he had earned about two hundred a year.

No questions were put on either side. The paintings were delivered at intervals, and the money received; and Priam knew no more. For many weeks he had lived in daily expectation of an uproar, a scandal in the art world, visits of police, and other inconveniences, for it was difficult to believe that the pictures would never come beneath the eye of a first-class expert. But nothing had occurred, and he had gradually subsided into a sense of security. He was happy; happy in the untrammelled exercise of his gift, happy in having all the money that his needs and Alice's demanded; happier than he had been in the errant days of his glory and his wealth. Alice had been amazed at his power of earning; and also, she had seemed little by little to lose her suspicions as to his perfect sanity and truthfulness. In a word, the dog of fate had slept; and he had taken particular care to let it lie. He was in that species of sheltered groove which is absolutely essential to the bliss of a shy and nervous artist, however great he may be.

And now this disastrous irruption, the resurrection of the early sins of the real Leek! He was hurt; he was startled; he was furious. But he was not surprised. The wonder was that the early sins of Henry Leek had not troubled him long ago. What could he do? He could do nothing. That was the tragedy: he could do nothing. He could but rely upon Alice. Alice was amazing. The more he thought of it, the more masterly her handling of those preposterous curates seemed to him. And was he to be robbed of this incomparable woman by ridiculous proceedings connected with a charge of bigamy? He knew that bigamy meant prison in England. The injustice was monstrous. He saw those curates, and their mute brother, and the aggrieved mother of the three dogging him either to prison or to his deathbed! And how could he explain to Alice? Impossible to explain to Alice! Still, it was conceivable that Alice would not desire explanation. Alice somehow never did desire an explanation. She always said, 'I can quite understand,' and set about preparing a meal. She was the comfortablest cushion of a creature that the evolution of the universe had ever produced.

Then the gusty breeze dropped and it began to rain. He ignored the rain. But December rain has a strange, horrid quality of chilly persistence. It is capable of conquering the most obstinate and serious mental preoccupation, and it conquered Priam's. It forced him to admit that his tortured soul had a fleshly garment, and that the fleshly garment was soaked to the marrow. And his soul gradually yielded before the attack of the rain, and he went home.

He put his latchkey into the door with minute precautions against noise, and crept into his house like a thief, and very gently shut the door. Then, in the hall, he intently listened. Not a sound! That is to say, not a sound except the drippings of his hat on the linoleum. The sitting-room door was ajar. He timidly pushed it, and entered. Alice was darning stockings.

'Henry!' she exclaimed. 'Why, you're wet through!' She rose.

'Have they cleared off?' he demanded.

'And you've been out without an overcoat! Henry how could you? Well, I must get you into bed at once – instantly, or I shall have you down with pneumonia or something to-morrow!'

'Have they cleared off?' he repeated.

'Yes, of course,' she said.

'When are they coming back?' he asked.

'I don't think they'll come back,' she replied. 'I think they've had enough. I think I've made them see that it's best to leave well alone. Did you ever see such toast as that curate made?'

'Alice, I assure you,' he said, later – he was in a boiling bath – 'I assure you it's all a mistake. I've never seen the woman before.'

'Of course you haven't,' she said calmingly. 'Of course you haven't. Besides, even if you had, it serves her right. Every one could see she's a nagging woman. And they seemed quite prosperous. They're hysterical – that's what's the matter with them, all of them – except the eldest, the one that never spoke. I rather liked him.'

'But I *haven't*!' he reiterated, splashing his positive statement into the water.

'My dear, I know you haven't.'

But he guessed that she was humouring him. He guessed that she was determined to keep him at all costs. And he had a disconcerting glimpse of the depths of utter unscrupulousness that sometimes disclose themselves in the mind of a good and loving woman.

'Only I hope there won't be any more of them!' she added dryly.

Ah! That was the point! He conceived the possibility of the rascal Leek having committed scores and scores of sins, all of which might come up against him. His affrighted vision saw whole regions ploughed by disconsolate widows of Henry Leek and their offspring, ecclesiastical and otherwise. He knew what Leek had been. Westminster Abbey was a strange goal for Leek to have achieved.

CHAPTER IX

A GLOSSY MALE

The machine was one of those electric contrivances that do their work noiselessly and efficiently, like a garrotter or the guillotine. No odour, no teeth-disturbing grind of rack-and-pinion, no trumpeting, with that machine! It arrived before the gate with such absence of sound that Alice, though she was dusting in the front-room, did not hear it. She heard nothing till the bell discreetly tinkled. Justifiably assuming that the tinkler was the butcher's boy, she went to the door with her apron on, and even with the duster in her hand. A handsome, smooth man stood on the step, and the electric carriage made a background for him. He was a dark man, with curly black hair, and a moustache to match, and black eyes. His silk hat, of an incredible smooth newness, glittered over his glittering hair and eyes. His overcoat was lined with astrakhan, and this important fact was casually betrayed at the lapels and at the sleeves. He wore a black silk necktie, with a small pearl pin in the mathematical centre of the perfect rhomboid of the upper part of a sailor's knot. His gloves were of slate colour. The chief characteristic of his faintly striped trousers was the crease, which seemed more than mortal. His boots were of *glacé* kid and as smooth as his cheeks. The cheeks had a fresh boyish colour, and between them, over admirable snowy teeth, projected the hooked key to his temperament. It is possible that Alice, from sheer thoughtlessness, shared the vulgar prejudice against Jews; but certainly she did not now feel it. The man's personal charm, his exceeding niceness, had always conquered that prejudice, whenever encountered. Moreover, he was only about thirty-five in years, and no such costly and beautiful male had ever yet stood on Alice's doorstep.

She at once, in her mind, contrasted him with the curates of the previous week, to the disadvantage of the Established Church. She did not know that this man was more dangerous than a thousand curates.

'Is this Mr Leek's?' he inquired smilingly, and raised his hat.

'Yes,' said Alice with a responsive smile.

'Is he in?'

'Well,' said Alice, 'he's busy at his work. You see, in this weather he can't go out much – not to work – and so he—'

'Could I see him in his studio?' asked the glossy man, with the air of saying, 'Can you grant me this supreme favour?'

It was the first time that Alice had heard the attic called a studio. She paused.

'It's about pictures,' explained the visitor.

'Oh!' said Alice. 'Will you come in?'

'I've run down specially to see Mr Leek,' said the visitor with emphasis.

Alice's opinion as to the seriousness of her husband's gift for painting had of course changed in two years. A man who can make two or three hundred a year by sticking colours anyhow, at any hazard, on canvases – by producing alleged pictures that in Alice's secret view bore only a comic resemblance to anything at all – that man had to be taken seriously in his attic as an artisan. It is true that Alice thought the payment he received miraculously high for the quality of the work done; but, with this agreeable Jew in the hall, and the *coupé* at the kerb, she suddenly perceived the probability of even greater miracles in the matter of price. She saw the average price of ten pounds rising to fifteen, or even twenty, pounds – provided her husband was given no opportunity to ruin the affair by his absurd, retiring shyness.

'Will you come this way?' she suggested briskly.

And all that elegance followed her up to the attic door: which door she threw open, remarking simply –

'Henry, here is a gentleman come to see you about pictures'

A CONNOISSEUR

Priam recovered more quickly than might have been expected. His first thought was naturally that women are uncalculated, if not incalculable, creatures, and that the best of them will do impossible things – things inconceivable till actually done! Fancy her introducing a stranger, without a word of warning, direct into his attic! However, when he rose he saw the visitor's nose (whose nostrils were delicately expanding and contracting in the fumes of the oil-stove), and he was at once reassured. He knew that he would have to face neither rudeness, nor bluntness, nor lack of imagination, nor lack of quick sympathy. Besides, the visitor, with practical assurance, set the tone of the interview instantly.

'Good morning, *maître*,' he began, right off. 'I must apologize for breaking in upon you. But I've come to see if you have any work to sell. My name is Oxford, and I'm acting for a collector.'

He said this with a very agreeable mingling of sincerity, deference, and mercantile directness, also with a bright, admiring smile. He showed no astonishment at the interior of the attic.

Maître!

Well, of course it would be idle to pretend that the greatest artists do not enjoy being addressed as *maître*. 'Master' is the same word, but entirely different. It was a long time since Priam Farll had been called *maître*. Indeed, owing to his retiring habit, he had very seldom been called *maître* at all. A just-finished picture stood on an easel near the window; it represented one of the most wonderful scenes in London: Putney High Street at night; two omnibus horses stepped strongly and willingly out of a dark side street, and under the cold glare of the main road they somehow took on the quality of equestrian sculpture. The alternation of lights was in the highest degree complex. Priam understood immediately, from the man's calm glance at the picture, and the position which he instinctively took up to see it, that he was accustomed to looking at pictures. The visitor did not start back, nor rush forward, nor dissolve into hysterics, nor behave as though confronted by the ghost of a murdered victim. He just gazed at the picture, keeping his nerve and holding his tongue. And yet it was not an easy picture to look at. It was a picture of an advanced experimentalism, and would have appealed to nothing but the sense of humour in a person not a connoisseur.

'Sell!' exclaimed Priam. Like all shy men he could hide his shyness in an exaggerated familiarity. 'What price this?' And he pointed to the picture. There were no other preliminaries.

'It is excessively distinguished,' murmured Mr Oxford, in the accents of expert appreciation. 'Excessively distinguished. May I ask how much?'

'That's what I'm asking you,' said Priam, fiddling with a paint-rag.

'Hum!' observed Mr Oxford, and gazed in silence. Then: 'Two hundred and fifty?'

Priam had virtually promised to deliver that picture to the picture-framer on the next day, and he had not expected to receive a penny more than twelve pounds for it. But artists are strange organisms.

He shook his head. Although two hundred and fifty pounds was as much as he had earned in the previous twelve months, he shook his grey head.

'No?' said Mr Oxford kindly and respectfully, putting his hands, behind his back. 'By the way,' he turned with eagerness to Priam, 'I presume you have seen the portrait of Ariosto by Titian that they've bought for the National Gallery? What is your opinion of it, *maître*?' He stood expectant, glowing with interest.

'Except that it isn't Ariosto, and it certainly isn't by Titian, it's a pretty high class sort of thing,' said Priam.

Mr Oxford smiled with appreciative content, nodding his head. 'I hoped you would say so,' he remarked. And swiftly he passed on to Segantini, then to J. W. Morrice, and then to Bonnard, demanding the *maître's* views. In a few moments they were really discussing pictures. And it was years since Priam had listened to the voice of informed common sense on the subject of painting. It was years since he had heard anything but exceeding puerility concerning pictures. He had, in fact, accustomed himself not to listen; he had excavated a passage direct from one ear to the other for such remarks. And now he drank up the conversation of Mr Oxford, and perceived that he had long been thirsty. And he spoke his mind. He grew warmer, more enthusiastic, more impassioned. And Mr Oxford listened with ecstasy. Mr Oxford had apparently a natural discretion. He simply accepted Priam, as he stood, for a great painter. No reference to the enigma why a great painter should be painting in an attic in Werter Road, Putney! No inconvenient queries about the great painter's previous history and productions. Just the frank, full acceptance of his genius! It was odd, but it was comfortable.

'So you won't take two hundred and fifty?' asked Mr Oxford, hopping back to business.

'No,' said Priam sturdily. 'The truth is,' he added, 'I should rather like to keep that picture for myself.'

'Will you take five hundred, *maître*?'

'Yes, I suppose I will,' and Priam sighed. A genuine sigh! For he would really have liked to keep the picture. He knew he had never painted a better.

'And may I carry it away with me?' asked Mr Oxford.

'I expect so,' said Priam.

'I wonder if I might venture to ask you to come back to town with me?' Mr Oxford went on, in gentle deference. 'I have one or two pictures I should very much like you to see, and I fancy they might give you pleasure. And we could talk over future business. If possibly you could spare an hour or so. If I might request—'

A desire arose in Priam's breast and fought against his timidity. The tone in which Mr Oxford had said, 'I fancy they might give you pleasure,' appeared to indicate something very much out of the common. And Priam could scarcely recollect when last his eyes had rested on a picture that was at once unfamiliar and great.

PARFITTS' GALLERIES

I have already indicated that the machine was somewhat out of the ordinary. It was, as a fact, exceedingly out of the ordinary. It was much larger than electric carriages usually are. It had what the writers of 'motoring notes' in papers written by the wealthy for the wealthy love to call a 'limousine body.' And outside and in, it was miraculously new and spotless. On the ivory handles of its doors, on its soft yellow leather upholstery, on its cedar woodwork, on its patent blind apparatus, on its silver fittings, on its lamps, on its foot-stools, on its silken arm-slings – not the minutest trace of usage! Mr Oxford's car seemed to show that Mr Oxford never used a car twice, purchasing a new car every morning, like stockbrokers

their silk hats, or the Duke of Selsea his trousers. There was a
table in the 'body' for writing, and pockets up and down
devised to hold documents, also two arm-chairs, and a
suspended contrivance which showed the hour, the temperature, and the fluctuations of the barometer; there was also a
speaking tube. One felt that if the machine had been connected
by wireless telegraphy with the Stock Exchange, the leading
studios and the Houses of Parliament, and if a little restaurant
had been constructed in the rear, Mr Oxford might never have
been under the necessity of leaving the car; that he might have
passed all his days in it from morn till latest eve.

The perfection of the machine and of Mr Oxford's attire and
complexion caused Priam to look rather shabby. Indeed, he
was rather shabby. Shabbiness had slightly overtaken him in
Putney. Once he had been a dandy; but that was in the
lamented Leek's time. And as the car glided, without smell
and without noise, through the encumbered avenues of London towards the centre, now shooting forward like a star,
now stopping with gentle suddenness, now swerving in a
swift curve round a vehicle earthy and leaden-wheeled, Priam
grew more and more uncomfortable. He had sunk into a
groove at Putney. He never left Putney, save occasionally to
refresh himself at the National Gallery, and thither he invariably went by train and tube, because the tube always filled
him with wonder and romance, and always threw him up out
of the earth at the corner of Trafalgar Square with such a
strange exhilaration in his soul. So that he had not seen the
main avenues of London for a long time. He had been
forgetting riches and luxury, and the oriental cigarette-shops
whose proprietors' names end in 'opoulos,' and the haughtiness of the ruling classes, and the still sterner haughtiness of
their footmen. He had now abandoned Alice in Putney. And a
mysterious demon seized him and gripped him, and sought to
pull him back in the direction of the simplicity of Putney, and
struggled with him fiercely, and made him writhe and shrink
before the brilliant phenomena of London's centre, and indeed
almost pitched him out of the car and set him running as hard
as legs would carry to Putney. It was the demon which we call
habit. He would have given a picture to be in Putney, instead
of swimming past Hyde Park Corner to the accompaniment

of Mr Oxford's amiable and deferential and tactful conversation.

However, his other demon, shyness, kept him from imperiously stopping the car.

The car stopped itself in Bond Street in front of a building with a wide archway, and the symbol of empire floating largely over its roof. Placards said that admission through the archway was a shilling; but Mr Oxford, bearing Priam's latest picture as though it had cost fifty thousand instead of five hundred pounds, went straight into the place without paying, and Priam accepted his impressive invitation to follow. Aged military veterans whose breasts carried a row of medals saluted Mr Oxford as he entered, and, within the penetralia, beings in silk hats as faultless as Mr Oxford's raised those hats to Mr Oxford, who did not raise his in reply. Merely nodded, Napoleonically! His demeanour had greatly changed. You saw here the man of unbending will, accustomed to use men as pawns in the chess of a complicated career. Presently they reached a private office where Mr Oxford, with the assistance of a page, removed his gloves, furs, and hat, and sent sharply for a man who at once brought a frame which fitted Priam's picture.

'Do have a cigar,' Mr Oxford urged Priam, with a quick return to his earlier manner, offering a box in which each cigar was separately encased in gold-leaf. The cigar was such as costs a crown in a restaurant, half a crown in a shop, and twopence in Amsterdam. It was a princely cigar, with the odour of paradise and an ash as white as snow. But Priam could not appreciate it. No! He had seen on a beaten copper plate under the archway these words: 'Parfitts' Galleries.' He was in the celebrated galleries of his former dealers, whom by the way he had never seen. And he was afraid. He was mortally apprehensive, and had a sickly sensation in the stomach.

After they had scrupulously inspected the picture, through the clouds of incense, Mr Oxford wrote out a cheque for five hundred pounds, and, cigar in mouth, handed it to Priam, who tried to take it with a casual air and did not succeed. It was signed 'Parfitts'.'

'I dare say you have heard that I'm now the sole proprietor of his place?' said Mr Oxford through his cigar.

'Really!' said Priam, feeling just as nervous as an inexper-
ienced youth.

Then Mr Oxford led Priam over thick carpets to a saloon
where electric light was thrown by means of reflectors on to a
small but incomparable band of pictures. Mr Oxford had not
exaggerated. They did give pleasure to Priam. They were not
the pictures one sees every day, nor once a year. There was the
finest Delacroix of its size that Priam had ever met with; also a
Vermeer that made it unnecessary to visit the Ryksmuseum.
And on the more distant wall, to which Mr Oxford came last,
in a place of marked honour, was an evening landscape of
Volterra, a hill-town in Italy. The bolts of Priam's very soul
started when he caught sight of that picture. On the lower
edge of the rich frame were two words in black lettering
'Priam Farll.' How well he remembered painting it! And how
masterfully beautiful it was!

'Now that,' said Mr Oxford, 'is in my humble opinion one
of the finest Farlls in existence. What do you think Mr Leek?'

Priam paused. 'I agree with you,' said he.

'Farll,' said Mr Oxford, 'is about the only modern painter
that can stand the company that that picture has in this room,
eh?'

Priam blushed. 'Yes,' he said.

There is a considerable difference, in various matters,
between Putney and Volterra; but the picture of Volterra and
the picture of Putney High Street were obviously, strikingly,
incontestably by the same hand; one could not but perceive the
same brushwork, the same masses, the same manner of seeing
and of grasping, in a word the same dazzling and austere
transition of nature. The resemblance jumped at one and
shook one by the shoulders. It could not have escaped even an
auctioneer. Yet Mr Oxford did not refer to it. He seemed
quite blind to it. All he said was, as they left the room, and
Priam finished his rather monosyllabic praise –

'Yes, that's the little collection I've just got together, and I
am very proud to have shown it to you. Now I want you to
come and lunch with me at my club. Please do. I should be
desolated if you refused.'

Priam did not care a halfpenny about the desolation of Mr
Oxford; and he most sincerely objected to lunch at Mr Oxford's

club. But he said 'Yes' because it was the easiest thing for his
shyness to do, Mr Oxford being a determined man. Priam was
afraid to go. He was disturbed, alarmed, affrighted by the
mystery of Mr Oxford's silence.

They arrived at the club in the car.

THE CLUB

Priam had never been in a club before. The statement may
astonish, may even meet with incredulity, but it is true. He
had left the land of clubs early in life. As for the English clubs
in European towns, he was familiar with their exteriors, and
with the amiable babble of their supporters at tables d'hôte,
and his desire for further knowledge had not been so hot as to
inconvenience him. Hence he knew nothing of clubs.

Mr Oxford's club alarmed and intimidated him; it was so
big and so black. Externally it resembled a town hall of some
great industrial town. As you stood on the pavement at the
bottom of the flight of giant steps that led to the first pair of
swinging doors, your head was certainly lower than the feet of
a being who examined you sternly from the other side of the
glass. Your head was also far below the sills of the mighty
windows of the ground-floor. There were two storeys above
the ground-floor, and above them a projecting eave of carven
stone that threatened the uplifted eye like a menace. The tenth
part of a slate, the merest chip of a corner, falling from the
lofty summit of that pile, would have slain elephants. And all
the façade was black, black with ages of carbonic deposit. The
notion that the building was a town hall that had got itself
misplaced and perverted gradually left you as you gazed. You
·perceived its falseness. You perceived that Mr Oxford's club
was a monument, a relic of the days when there were giants on
earth, that it had come down unimpaired to a race of pigmies,
who were making the best of it. The sole descendant of the
giants was the scout behind the door. As Mr Oxford and
Priam climbed towards it, this unique giant, with a giant's
force, pulled open the gigantic door, and Mr Oxford and
Priam walked imperceptibly in, and the door swung to with a
large displacement of air. Priam found himself in an immense

interior, under a distant carved ceiling, far, far upwards, like heaven. He watched Mr Oxford write his name in a gigantic folio, under a gigantic clock. This accomplished, Mr Oxford led him past enormous vistas to right and left, into a very long chamber, both of whose long walls were studded with thousands upon thousands of massive hooks – and here and there upon a hook a silk hat or an overcoat. Mr Oxford chose a couple of hooks in the expanse, and when they had divested themselves sufficiently he led Priam forwards into another great chamber evidently meant to recall the baths of Caracalla. In gigantic basins chiselled out of solid granite, Priam scrubbed his finger-nails with a nail-brush larger then he had previously encountered, even in nightmares, and an attendant brushed his coat with a utensil that resembled a weapon of offence lately the property of Anak.

'Shall we go straight to the dining-room now,' asked Mr Oxford, 'or will you have a gin and angostura first?'

Priam declined the gin and angostura, and they went up an overwhelming staircase of sombre marble, and through other apartments to the dining-room, which would have made an excellent riding-school. Here one had six of the gigantic windows in a row, each with curtains that fell in huge folds from the unseen into the seen. The ceiling probably existed. On every wall were gigantic paintings in thick ornate frames, and between the windows stood heroic busts of marble set upon columns of basalt. The chairs would have been immovable had they not run on castors of weight-resisting rock, yet against the tables they had the air of negligible toys. At one end of the room was a sideboard that would not have groaned under an ox whole, and at the other a fire, over which an ox might have been roasted in its entirety, leaped under a mantelpiece upon which Goliath could not have put his elbows.

All was silent and grave; the floors were everywhere covered with heavy carpets which hushed all echoes. There was not the faintest sound. Sound, indeed, seemed to be deprecated. Priam had already passed the wide entrance to one illimitable room whose walls were clothed with warnings in gigantic letters: 'Silence.' And he had noticed that all chairs and couches were thickly padded and upholstered in soft leather, and that it was impossible to produce in them the slightest creak. At a casual glance the place seemed unoccupied, but on more careful inspection you saw midgets creeping about, or seated in easy chairs that had obviously been made to hold two of them; these midgets were the members of the club, dwarfed into dolls by its tremendous dimensions. A strange and sinister race! They looked as though in the final stages of decay, and wherever their heads might rest was stretched a white cloth, so that their heads might not touch the spots sanctified by the heads of the mighty departed. They rarely spoke to one another, but exchanged regards of mutual distrust and scorn; and if by chance they did converse it was in tones of weary, brusque disillusion. They could at best descry each other but indistinctly in the universal pervading gloom – a gloom upon which electric lamps, shining dimly yellow in their vast lustres, produced almost no impression. The whole establishment was buried in the past, dreaming of its Titanic yore, when there were doubtless giants who could fill those fauteuils and stick their feet on those mantelpieces.

It was in such an environment that Mr Oxford gave Priam to eat and to drink off little ordinary plates and out of tiny tumblers. No hint of the club's immemorial history in that excessively modern and excellent repast – save in the Stilton cheese, which seemed to have descended from the fine fruity days of some Homeric age, a cheese that Ulysses might have inaugurated. I need hardly say that the total effect on Priam's temperament was disastrous. (Yet how could the diplomatic Mr Oxford have guessed that Priam had never been in a club before?) It induced in him a speechless anguish, and he would have paid a sum as gigantic as the club – he would have paid the very cheque in his pocket – never to have met Mr Oxford. He was a far too sensitive man for a club, and his moods were incalculable. Assuredly Mr Oxford had miscalculated the result of his club on Priam's humour; he soon saw his error.

'Suppose we take coffee in the smoking-room?' he said.

The populous smoking-room was the one part of the club where talking with a natural loudness was not a crime. Mr Oxford found a corner fairly free from midgets, and they established themselves in it, and liqueurs and cigars accompanied the coffee. You could actually see midgets laughing outright in the mist of smoke; the chatter narrowly escaped being a din; and at intervals a diminutive boy entered and bawled the name of a midget at the top of his voice. Priam was suddenly electrified and Mr Oxford, very alert, noticed the electrification.

Mr Oxford drank his coffee somewhat quickly, and then he leaned forward a little over the table, and put his moon-like face nearer to Priam's, and arranged his legs in a truly comfortable position beneath the table, and expelled a large quantity of smoke from his cigar. It was clearly the preliminary to a scene of confidence, the approach to the crisis to which he had for several hours been leading up.

Priam's heart trembled.

'What is your opinion, *maître*,' he asked, 'of the ultimate value of Farll's pictures?'

Priam was in misery. Mr Oxford's manner was deferential, amiable, and expectant. But Priam did not know what to say. He only knew what he would do if he could have found the courage to do it: run away, recklessly, unceremoniously, out of that club.

'I – I don't know,' said Priam, visibly whitening.

'Because I've bought a goodish few Farlls in my time,' Mr Oxford continued, 'and I must say I've sold them well. I've only got that one left that I showed you this morning, and I've been wondering whether I should stick to it for a possible further rise, or sell it at once.'

'How much can you sell it for?' Priam mumbled.

'I don't mind telling you,' said Mr Oxford, 'that I fancy I could sell it for a couple of thousand. It's rather small, but it's one of the finest in existence.'

'I should sell it,' said Priam, scarcely audible.

'You would? Well, perhaps you're right. It's a question, in my mind, whether some other painter may not turn up one of these days who would do that sort of thing even better than Farll did it. I could imagine the possibility of a really clever man coming along and imitating Farll so well that only people like yourself, *maître*, and perhaps me, could tell the difference. It's just the kind of work that might be brilliantly imitated, if the imitator was clever enough, don't you think?'

'But what do you mean?' asked Priam, perspiring in his back.

'Well,' said Mr Oxford vaguely, 'one never knows. The style might be imitated, and the market flooded with canvases practically as good as Farll's. Nobody might find it out for quite a long time, and then there might be confusion in the public mind, followed by a sharp fall in prices. And the beauty of it is that the public wouldn't really be any the worse. Because an imitation that no one can distinguish from the original is naturally as good as the original. You take me? There's certainly a tremendous chance for a man who could seize it, and that's why I'm inclined to accept your advice and sell my one remaining Farll.'

He smiled more and more confidentially. His gaze was charged with a secret meaning. He seemed to be suggesting unspeakable matters to Priam. That bright face wore an expression which such faces wear on such occasions – an expression cheerfully insinuating that after all there is no right and no wrong – or at least that many things which the ordinary slave of convention would consider to be wrong are really right. So Priam read the expression.

'The dirty rascal wants me to manufacture imitations of myself for him!' Priam thought, full of sudden, hidden anger. 'He's known all along that there's no difference between what I sold him and the picture he's already had. He wants to suggest that we should come to terms. He's simply been playing a game with me up to now.' And he said aloud, 'I don't know that I *advise* you to do anything. I'm not a dealer, Mr Oxford.'

He said it in a hostile tone that ought to have silenced Mr Oxford for ever, but it did not. Mr Oxford curved away, like a skater into a new figure, and began to expatiate minutely upon the merits of the Volterra picture. He analysed it in so much detail, and lauded it with as much justice, as though the picture was there before them. Priam was astonished at the man's exactitude. 'Scoundrel! He knows a thing or two!' reflected Priam grimly.

'You don't think I overpraise it, do you, *cher maître?*' Mr Oxford finished, still smiling.

'A little,' said Priam.

If only Priam could have run away! But he couldn't! Mr Oxford had him well in a corner. No chance of freedom! Besides, he was over fifty, and stout.

'Ah!' Now, I was expecting you to say that! Do you mind telling me at what period you painted it?' Mr Oxford inquired, very blandly, though his hands were clasped in a violent tension that forced the blood from the regions of the knuckle-joints.

This was the crisis which Mr Oxford had been leading up to! All the time Mr Oxford's teethy smile had concealed a knowledge of Priam's identity!

CHAPTER X

THE SECRET

'What do you mean?' asked Priam Farll. But he put the question weakly, and he might just as well have said, 'I know what you mean, and I would pay a million pounds or so in order to sink through the floor.' A few minutes ago he would only have paid five hundred pounds or so in order to run simply away. Now he wanted Maskelyne miracles to happen to him. The universe seemed to be caving in about the ears of Priam Farll.

Mr Oxford was still smiling; smiling, however, as a man holds his breath for a wager. You felt that he could not keep it up much longer.

'You *are* Priam Farll, aren't you?' said Mr Oxford in a very low voice.

'What makes you think I'm Priam Farll?'

'I think you are Priam Farll because you painted that picture I bought from you this morning, and I am sure that no one but Priam Farll could have painted it.'

'Then you've been playing a game with me all the morning?'

'Please don't put it like that, *cher maître*,' Mr Oxford whisperingly pleaded. 'I only wish to feel my ground. I know that Priam Farll is supposed to have been buried in Westminster Abbey. But for me the existence of that picture of Putney High Street, obviously just painted, is an absolute proof that he is not buried in Westminster Abbey, and that he still lives. It is an amazing thing that there should have been a mistake at the funeral, an utterly amazing thing, which involves all sorts of consequences! But that's not my business. Of course there must be clear reasons for what occurred. I am not interested in them – I mean not professionally. I merely argue, when I see a certain picture, with the paint still wet on it: "That picture was painted by a certain painter. I am an expert, and I stake my reputation on it." It's no use telling me that the painter in question died several years ago and was buried with national honours in Westminster Abbey. I say it couldn't have been so. I'm a connoisseur. And if the facts of his death and burial don't agree with the result of my connoisseurship, I say they aren't facts. I say there's been a – a misunderstanding about – er – corpses. Now, *cher maître*, what do you think of my position?' Mr Oxford drummed lightly on the table.

'I don't know,' said Priam. Which was another lie.

'You *are* Priam Farll, aren't you?' Mr Oxford persisted.

'Well, if you will have it,' said Priam savagely, 'I am. And now you know!'

Mr Oxford let his smile go. He had held it for an incredible time. He let it go, and sighed a gentle and profound relief. He had been skating over the thinnest ice, and had reached the bank amid terrific cracklings, and he began to appreciate the extent of the peril braved. He had been perfectly sure of his connoisseurship. But when one says one is perfectly sure, especially if one says it with immense emphasis, one always means 'Imperfectly sure.' So it was with Mr Oxford. And really, to argue, from the mere existence of a picture, that a tremendous deceit had been successfully practised upon the most formidable of nations, implies rather more than rashness on the part of the arguer.

'But I don't want it to get about,' said Priam, still in a savage whisper. 'And I don't want to talk about it.' He looked at the nearest midget, resentfully suspecting them of eavesdropping.

'Precisely,' said Mr Oxford, but in a tone that lacked conviction.

'It's a matter that only concerns me,' said Priam.

'Precisely,' Mr Oxford repeated. 'At least it *ought* to concern only you. And I can't assure you too positively that I'm the last person in the world to want to pry; but—'

'You must kindly remember,' said Priam, interrupting, 'that you bought that picture this morning simply *as* a picture, on its merits. You have no authority to attach my name to it, and I must ask you not to do so.'

'Certainly,' agreed Mr Oxford. 'I bought it as a master-piece, and I'm quite content with my bargain. I want no signature.'

'I haven't signed my pictures for twenty years,' said Priam.

'Pardon me,' said Mr Oxford. 'Every square inch of every one is unmistakably signed. You could not put a brush on a canvas without signing it. It is the privilege of only the greatest painters not to put letters on the corners of their pictures, in order to keep other painters from taking the credit for them afterwards. For me, all your pictures are signed. But there are some people who want more proof than connois-seurship can give, and that's where the trouble is going to be.'

'Trouble?' said Priam, with an intensification of his misery.

'Yes,' said Mr Oxford. 'I must tell you, so that you can understand the situation.' He became very solemn, showing that he had at last reached the real point. 'Some time ago a man, a little dealer, came to me and offered me a picture that I instantly recognized as one of yours. I bought it.'

'How much did you pay for it?' Priam growled.

After a pause, Mr Oxford said, 'I don't mind giving you the figure. I paid fifty pounds for it.'

'Did you!' exclaimed Priam, perceiving that some person or persons had made four hundred per cent on his work by the time it had arrived at a big dealer. 'Who was the fellow?'

'Oh, a little dealer. Nobody. Jew, of course.' Mr Oxford's way of saying 'Jew' was ineffably ironic. Priam knew that, being a Jew, the dealer could not be his frame-maker, who was a pure-bred Yorkshireman from Ravensthorpe. Mr Oxford continued, 'I sold that picture and guaranteed it to be a Priam Farll.'

'The devil you did!'

'Yes. I had sufficient confidence in my judgement.'

'Who bought it?'

'Whitney C. Witt, of New York. He's an old man now, of course. I expect you remember him, *cher maître*.' Mr Oxford's eyes twinkled. 'I sold it to him, and of course he accepted my guarantee. Soon afterwards I had the offer of other pictures obviously by you, from the same dealer. And I bought them. I kept on buying them. I dare say I've bought forty altogether.'

'Did your little dealer guess whose work they were?' Priam demanded suspiciously.

'Not he! If he had done, do you suppose he'd have parted with them for fifty pounds apiece. Mind, at first I thought I was buying pictures painted before your supposed death. I thought, like the rest of the world, that you were – in the Abbey. Then I began to have doubts. And one day when a bit of paint came off on my thumb, I can tell you I was startled. However, I stuck to my opinion, and I kept on guaranteeing the pictures as Farlls.'

'It never occurred to you to make any inquiries?'

'Yes, it did,' said Mr Oxford. 'I did my best to find out from the dealer where he got the pictures from, but he wouldn't tell me. Well, I sort of scented a mystery. Now, I've got no professional use for mysteries, and I came to the conclusion that I'd better just let this one alone. So I did.'

'Well, why don't you keep on leaving it alone?' Priam asked.

'Because circumstances won't let me. I sold practically all those pictures to Whitney C. Witt. It was all right. Anyhow, I thought it was all right. I put Parfitts' name and reputation on their being yours. And then one day I heard from Mr Witt that on the back of the canvas of one of the pictures the name of the canvas-makers, and a date, had been stamped with a rubber stamp, and that the date was after your supposed burial, and that his London solicitors had made inquiries from the artist's-material people here, and these people were prepared to prove that the canvas was made after Priam Farll's funeral. You see the fix?'

Priam did.

'My reputation – Parfitts' – is at stake. If those pictures aren't by you, I'm a swindler. Parfitts' name is gone for ever, and there'll be the greatest scandal that ever was. Witt is threatening proceedings. I offered to take the whole lot back at the price he paid me, without any commission. But he won't. He's an old man; a bit of a maniac, I expect, and he won't. He's angry. He thinks he's been swindled, and what he says is that he's going to see the thing through. I've got to prove to him that the pictures are yours. I've got to show him what grounds I had for giving my guarantee. Well, to cut a long story short, I've found you, I'm glad to say!'

He sighed again.

'Look here,' said Priam. 'How much has Witt paid you altogether for my pictures?'

After a pause, Mr Oxford said, 'I don't mind giving you the figure. He's paid me seventy-two thousand pounds odd.' He smiled, as if to excuse himself.

When Priam Farll reflected that he had received about four hundred pounds for those pictures – vastly less than one per cent of what the shiny and prosperous dealer had ultimately disposed of them for, the traditional fury of the artist against the dealer – of the producer against the parasitic middleman – sprang into flame in his heart. Up till then he had never had any serious cause of complaint against his dealers. (Extremely successful artists seldom have.) Now he saw dealers, as the ordinary painters see them, to be the authors of all evil! Now he understood by what methods Mr Oxford had achieved his splendid car, clothes, club, and minions. These things were earned, not by Mr Oxford, but *for* Mr Oxford in dingy studios, even in attics, by shabby industrious painters! Mr Oxford was nothing but an opulent thief, a grinder of the face of genius. Mr Oxford was, in a word, the spawn of the devil, and Priam silently but sincerely consigned him to his proper place.

It was excessively unjust of Priam. Nobody had asked Priam to die. Nobody had asked him to give up his identity. If he had latterly been receiving tens instead of thousands for his pictures, the fault was his alone. Mr Oxford had only bought and only sold; which was his true function. But Mr Oxford's sin in Priam's eyes, was the sin of having been right.

It would have needed less insight than Mr Oxford had at his disposal to see that Priam Farll was taking the news very badly.

'For both our sakes, *cher maître*,' said Mr Oxford persuasively, 'I think it will be advisable for you to put me in a
position to prove that my guarantee to Witt was justified.'

'Why for both our sakes?'

'Because, well, I shall be delighted to pay you, say thirty-six
thousand pounds in acknowledgement of – er —' He stopped.

Probably he had instantly perceived that he was committing
a disastrous error of fact. Either he should have offered
nothing, or he should have offered the whole sum he had
received less a small commission. To suggest dividing equally
with Priam was the instinctive impulse, the fatal folly, of a
born dealer. And Mr Oxford was a born dealer.

'I won't accept a penny,' said Priam. 'And I can't help you
in any way. I'm afraid I must go now. I'm late as it is.'

His cold, resistless fury drove him forward, and without the
slightest regard for the amenities of clubs, he left the table.

Mr Oxford, becoming more and more the dealer, rose and
followed him, even directed him to the gigantic cloak-room,
murmuring the while soft persuasions and pacifications in
Priam's ear.

'There may be an action in the courts,' said Mr Oxford in
the grand entrance hall, 'and your testimony would be
indispensable to me.'

'I can have nothing to do with it. Good day!'

The giant at the door could scarce open the gigantic portal
quickly enough for him. He fled – fled, surrounded by
nightmare visions of horrible publicity in a law-court.
Unthinkable tortures! He damned Mr Oxford to the nether-
most places, and swore that he would not lift a finger to save
Mr Oxford from penal servitude for life.

MONEY-GETTING

He stood on the kerb of the monument, talking to himself
savagely. At any rate he was safely outside the monument,
with its pullulating population of midgets creeping over its
carpets and lounging insignificantly on its couches. He could
not remember clearly what had occurred since the moment òf
his getting up from the table; he could not remember seeing

anything or any one on his way out; but he could remember
the persuasive, deferential voice of Mr Oxford following him
persistently as far as the giant's door. In recollection that club
was like an abode of black magic to him; it seemed so
hideously alive in its deadness, and its doings were so absurd
and mysterious – 'Silence, silence!' commanded the white
papers in one vast chamber, and, in another, babel existed!
And then that terrible mute dining-room, with the high,
unscalable mantelpieces that no midget could ever reach!

He kept uttering the most dreadful judgments on the club
and on Mr Oxford, in quite audible tones, oblivious of the
street. He was aroused by a rather scared man saluting him. It
was Mr Oxford's chauffeur, waiting patiently till his master
should be ready to re-enter the wheeled salon. The chauffeur
apparently thought him either demented or inebriated, but his
sole duty was to salute, and he did nothing else.

Quite forgetting that this chauffeur was a fellow-creature,
Priam immediately turned upon his heel, and hurried down
the street. At the corner of the street was a large bank, and
Priam, acquiring the reckless courage of the soldier in battle,
entered the bank. He had never been in a London bank before.

At first it reminded him of the club, with the addition of an
enormous placard giving the day of the month as a mystical
number – 14 – and other placards displaying solitary letters of
the alphabet. Then he saw that it was a huge menagerie in
which highly trained young men of assorted sizes and years
were confined in stout cages of wire and mahogany. He
stamped straight to a cage with a hole in it, and threw down
the cheque for five hundred pounds – defiantly.

'Next desk, please,' said a mouth over a high collar and a
green tie, behind the grating, and a disdainful hand pushed the
cheque back towards Priam.

'Next desk!' repeated Priam, dashed but furious.

'This is the A to M desk,' said the mouth.

Then Priam understood the solitary letters, and he rushed,
with a new accession of fury, to the adjoining cage, where
another disdainful hand picked up the cheque and turned it
over, with an air of saying, 'Fishy, this!'

And, 'It isn't endorsed!' said another mouth over another
high collar and green tie. The second disdainful hand pushed

the cheque back again to Priam, as though it had been a begging circular.

'Oh, if that's all!' said Priam, who could scarcely speak from anger. 'Have you got such a thing as a pen?'

He was behaving in an extremely unreasonable manner. He had no right to visit his spleen on a perfectly innocent bank that paid twenty-five per cent to its shareholders and a thousand a year each to its directors, and what trifle was left over to its men in cages. But Priam was not like you or me. He did not invariably act according to reason. He could not be angry with one man at once, nor even with one building at once. When he was angry he was inclusively and miscel-laneously angry; and the sun, moon, and stars did not escape.

After he had endorsed the cheque the disdainful hand clawed it up once more, and directed upon its obverse and upon its reverse a battery of suspicions; then a pair of eyes glanced with critical distrust at so much of Priam's person as was visible. Then the eyes moved back, the mouth opened, and a brief word, and lo! there were four eyes and two mouths over the cheque, and four eyes for an instant on Priam. Priam expected some one to call for a policeman; in spite of himself he felt guilty – or anyhow dubious. It was the grossest insult to him to throw doubt on the cheque and to examine him in that frigid, shamelessly disillusioned manner.

'You *are* Mr Leek?' a mouth moved.

'Yes' (very slowly).

'How would you like this?'

'I'll thank you to give it me in notes,' answered Priam haughtily.

When the disdainful hand had counted twice every corner of a pile of notes, and had dropped the notes one by one, with a peculiar snapping sound of paper, in front of Priam, Priam crushed them together and crammed them, without any ceremony and without gratitude to the giver, into the right pocket of his trousers. And he stamped out of the building with curses on his lips.

Still, he felt better, he felt assuaged. To cultivate and nourish a grievance when you have five hundred pounds in your pocket, in cash, is the most difficult thing in the world.

A VISIT TO THE TAILOR'S

He gradually grew calmer by dint of walking – aimless, fast
walking, with a rapt expression of the eyes that on crowded
pavements cleared the way for him more effectually than a
shouting footman. And then he debouched unexpectedly on
to the Embankment. Dusk was already falling on the noble
curve of the Thames and the mighty panorama stretched
before him in a manner mysteriously impressive, which has
made poets of less poetic men than Priam Farll. Grand
hotels, offices of millionaires and of governments, grand
hotels, swards and mullioned windows of the law, grand
hotels, the terrific arches of termini, cathedral domes, houses
of parliament, and grand hotels, rose darkly around him on
the arc of the river, against the dark violent murk of the sky.
Huge trams swam past him like glass houses, and hansoms
shot past the trams and automobiles past the hansoms; and
phantom barges swirled down on the full ebb, threading
holes in bridges as cotton threads a needle. It was London,
and the roar of London, majestic, imperial, super-Roman.
And lo! earlier than the earliest municipal light, an unseen
hand, the hand of destiny, printed a writing on the wall of
vague gloom that was beginning to hide the opposite bank.
And the writing said that Shipton's tea was the best. And
then the hand wiped largely out that message and wrote in
another spot that Macdonnell's whiskey was the best; and so
these two doctrines, in their intermittent pyrotechnics, continued to give the lie to each other under the deepening
night. Quite five minutes passed before Priam perceived,
between the altercating doctrines, the high scaffold-clad
summit of a building which was unfamiliar to him. It looked
serenely and immaterially beautiful in the evening twilight,
and as he was close to Waterloo Bridge, his curiosity concerning beauty took him over to the south bank of the
Thames.

After losing himself in the purlieus of Waterloo Station, he
at last discovered the rear of the building. Yes, it was a
beautiful thing; its tower climbed in several coloured storeys,
diminishing till it expired in a winged figure on the sky. And

below, the building was broad and massive, with a frontage of pillars over great arched windows. Two cranes stuck their arms out from the general mass, and the whole enterprise was guarded in a hedge of hoardings. Through the narrow doorway in the hoarding came the flare and the hissing of a Well's light. Priam Farll glanced timidly within. The interior was immense. In a sort of court of honour a group of muscular, hairy males, silhouetted against an illuminated latticework of scaffolding, were chipping and paring at huge blocks of stone. It was a subject for a Rembrandt.

A fat, untidy man meditatively approached the doorway. He had a roll of tracing papers in his hand, and the end of a long, thick pencil in his mouth. He was the man who interpreted the dreams of the architect to the dreamy British artisan. Experience of life had made him somewhat brusque.

'Look here,' he said to Priam; 'what the devil do you want?'

'What the devil do I want?' repeated Priam, who had not yet altogether fallen away from his mode of universal defiance. 'I only want to know what the h—ll this building is.'

The fat man was a little startled. He took his pencil from his mouth, and spat.

'It's the new Picture Gallery, built under the will of that there Priam Farll. I should ha' thought you'd ha' known that.' Priam's lips trembled on the verge of an exclamation. 'See that?' the fat man pursued, pointing to a small board on the hoarding. The board said, 'No hands wanted.'

The fat man coldly scrutinized Priam's appearance, from his greenish hat to his baggy creased boots.

Priam walked away.

He was dumbfounded. Then he was furious again. He perfectly saw the humour of the situation, but it was not the kind of humour that induced rollicking laughter. He was furious, and employed the language of fury, when it is not overheard. Absorbed by his craft of painting, as in the old Continental days, he had long since ceased to read the newspapers, and though he had not forgotten his bequest to the nation, he had never thought of it as taking architectural shape. He was not aware of his cousin Duncan's activities for the perpetuation of the family name. The thing staggered him. The probabilities of the strange consequences of dead actions swept against him and overwhelmed him. Once, years ago, and years ago, in a resentful mood, he had written a few lines on a piece of paper, and signed them in the presence of witnesses. Then nothing – nothing whatever – for two decades! The paper slept . . . and now this – this tremendous concrete result in the heart of London! It was incredible. It passed the bounds even of lawful magic.

His palace, his museum! The fruit of a captious hour! Ah! But he was furious. Like every ageing artist of genuine accomplishment, he knew – none better – that there is no satisfaction save the satisfaction of fatigue after honest endeavour. He knew – none better – that wealth and glory and fine clothes are nought, and that striving is all. He had never been happier than during the last two years. Yet the finest souls have their reactions, their rebellions against wise reason. And Priam's soul was in insurrection then. He wanted wealth and glory and fine clothes once more. It seemed to him that he was out of the world and that he must return to it. The covert insults of Mr Oxford rankled and stung. And the fat foreman had mistaken him for a workman cadging for a job.

He walked rapidly to the bridge and took a cab to Conduit Street, where dwelt a firm of tailors with whose Paris branch he had had dealings in his dandiacal past.

And odd impulse perhaps, but natural.

A lighted clock-tower – far to his left as the cab rolled across the bridge – showed that a legislative providence was watching over Israel.

ALICE ON THE SITUATION

'I bet the building alone won't cost less then seventy thousand pounds,' he said.

He was back again with Alice in the intimacy of Werter Road, and relating to her, in part, the adventures of the latter portion of the day. He had reached home long after tea-time; she, with her natural sagacity, had not waited tea for him. Now she had prepared a rather special tea for the adventurer, and she was sitting opposite to him at the little table, with nothing to do but listen and refill his cup.

'Well,' she said mildly, and without the least surprise at his figures, 'I don't know what he could have been thinking of – your Priam Farll! I call it just silly. It isn't as if there wasn't enough picture galleries already. When what there are are so full that you can't get in – then it will be time enough to think about fresh ones. I've been to the National Gallery twice, and upon my word, I was almost the only person there! And it's free too! – People don't *want* picture galleries. If they did they'd go. Who ever saw a public-house empty, or Peter Robinson's? And you have to pay there! Silly, I call it! Why couldn't he have left his money to you, or at any rate to the hospitals, or something of that? No, it isn't silly. It's scandalous. It ought to be stopped!'

Now Priam had resolved that evening to make a serious, gallant attempt to convince his wife of his own identity. He was approaching the critical point. This speech of hers intimidated him, rather complicated his difficulties, but he determined to proceed bravely.

'Have you put sugar in this?' he asked.

'Yes,' she said. 'But you've forgotten to stir it. I'll stir it for you.'

A charming wifely attention! It enheartened him.

'I say, Alice,' he said, as she stirred, 'you remember when first I told you I could paint?'

'Yes,' she said.

'Well, at first you thought I was daft. You thought my mind was wandering, didn't you?'

'No,' she said, 'I only thought you'd got a bee in your bonnet.' She smiled demurely.

'Well, I hadn't, had I?'

'Seeing the money you've made, I should just say you hadn't,' she handsomely admitted. 'Where we should be without it I don't know.'

'You were wrong, weren't you? And I was right?'

'Of course,' she beamed.

'And do you remember that time I told you I was really Priam Farll?'

She nodded reluctantly.

'You thought I was absolutely mad. Oh, you needn't deny it! I could see well enough what your thoughts were.'

'I thought you weren't quite well,' she said frankly.

'But I was, my child. Now, I've got to tell you again that I am Priam Farll. Honestly I wish I wasn't, but I am. The deuce of it is that that fellow that came here this morning has found it out, and there's going to be trouble. At least there has been trouble, and there may be more.'

She was impressed. She knew not what to say.

'But, Priam—'

'He's paid me five hundred pounds to-day for that picture I've just finished.'

'Five hund—'

Priam snatched the notes from his pocket, and with a gesture pardonably dramatic he bade her count them.

'Count them,' he repeated, when she hesitated.

'Is it right?' he asked when she had finished.

'Oh, it's right enough,' she agreed. 'But, Priam, I don't like having all this money in the house. You ought to have called and put it in the bank.'

'Dash the bank!' he exclaimed. 'Just keep on listening to me, and try to persuade yourself I'm not mad. I admit I'm a bit shy, and it was all on account of that that I let that d—d valet of mine be buried as me.'

'You needn't tell me you're shy,' she smiled. 'All Putney knows you're shy.'

'I'm not so sure about that!' He tossed his head.

Then he began at the beginning and recounted to her in detail the historic night and morning at Selwood Terrace, with a psychological description of his feelings. He convinced her in less than ten minutes, with the powerful aid of five hundred pounds in bank-notes, that he in truth was Priam Farll.

And he waited for her to express an exceeding astonishment and satisfaction.

'Well, of course if you are, you are,' she observed simply, regarding him with benevolent, possessive glances across the table. The fact was that she did not deal in names, she dealt in realities. He was her reality, and so long as he did not change visibly or actually – so long as he remained he – she did not much mind who he was. She added, 'But I really don't know what you were *dreaming* of, Henry, to do such a thing!'

'Neither do I,' he muttered.

Then he disclosed to her the whole chicanery of Mr Oxford.

'It's a good thing you've ordered those new clothes,' she said.

'Why?'

'Because of the trial.'

The trial between Oxford and Witt. What's that got to do with me?'

'They'll make you give evidence.'

'But I shan't give evidence. I've told Oxford I'll have nothing to do with it at all.'

'Suppose they make you? They can, you know, with a sub – sub something, I forget it's name. Then you'll *have* to go in the witness-box.'

'Me in the witness-box!' he murmured, undone.

'Yes,' she said. 'I expect it'll be very provoking indeed. But you'd want a new suit for it. So I'm glad you ordered one. When are you going to try it on?'

CHAPTER XI

AN ESCAPE

One night in the following June, Priam and Alice refrained from going to bed. Alice dozed for an hour or so on the sofa, and Priam read by her side in an easychair, and about two o'clock, just before the first beginnings of dawn, they stimulated themselves into a feverish activity beneath the parlour gas. Alice prepared tea, bread and butter, and eggs, passing briskly from room to room. Alice also ran upstairs, cast a few more things into a valise and a bag already partially packed, and, locking both receptacles, carried them downstairs. Meantime the whole of Priam's energy was employed in having a bath and in shaving. Blood was shed, as was but natural at that ineffable hour. While Priam consumed the food she had prepared, Alice was continually darting to and fro in the house. At one moment, after an absence, she would come into the parlour with a mouthful of hatpins; at another she

would rush out to assure herself that the indispensable keys of
the valise and bag with her purse were on the umbrella-stand,
where they could not be forgotten. Between her excursions
she would drink thirty drops of tea.

'Now, Priam,' she said at length, 'the water's hot. Haven't
you finished? It'll be getting light soon.'

'Water hot?' he queried, at a loss.

'Yes,' she said. 'To wash up these things, of course. You
don't suppose I'm going to leave a lot of dirty things in the
house, do you? While I'm doing that you might stick labels on
the luggage.'

'They won't need to be labelled,' he argued. 'We shall take
them with us in the carriage.'

'Oh, Priam,' she protested, 'how tiresome you are!'

'I've travelled more than you have.' He tried to laugh.

'Yes, and fine travelling it must have been, too! However, if
you don't mind the luggage being lost, I don't.'

During this she was collecting the crockery on a tray, with
which tray she whizzed out of the room.

In ten minutes, hatted, heavily veiled, and gloved, she
cautiously opened the front door and peeped forth into the
lamplit street. She peered to right and to left. Then she went as
far as the gate and peered again.

'Is it all right?' whispered Priam, who was behind her.

'Yes, I think so,' she whispered.

Priam came out of the house with the bag in one hand and
the valise in the other, a pipe in his mouth, a stick under his
arm, and an overcoat on his shoulder. Alice ran up the steps,
gazed within the house, pulled the door to silently, and locked
it. Then beneath the summer stars she and Priam hastened
furtively, as though the luggage had contained swag, up
Werter Road towards Oxford Road. When they had turned
the corner they felt very much relieved.

They had escaped.

It was their second attempt. The first, made in daylight, had
completely failed. Their cab had been followed to Paddington
Station by three other cabs containing the representatives and
the cameras of three Sunday newspapers. A journalist had
deliberately accompanied Priam to the booking-office, had
heard him ask for two seconds to Weymouth, and had bought

a second to Weymouth himself. They had gone to Weymouth, but as within two hours of their arrival Weymouth had become even more impossible than Werter Road, they had ignominiously but wisely come back.

Werter Road had developed into the most celebrated thoroughfare in London. Its photograph had appeared in scores of newspapers, with a cross marking the abode of Priam and Alice. It was beset and infested by journalists of several nationalities from morn till night. Cameras were as common in it as lamp-posts. And a famous descriptive reporter of the 'Sunday News' had got lodgings, at a high figure, exactly opposite No. 29. Priam and Alice could do nothing without publicity. And if it would be an exaggeration to assert that evening papers appeared with Stop-press News: '5.40 Mrs Leek went out shopping,' the exaggeration would not be very extravagant. For a fortnight Priam had not been beyond the door during daylight. It was Alice who, alarmed by Priam's pallid cheeks and tightened nerves, had devised the plan of flight before the early summer dawn.

They reached East Putney Station, of which the gates were closed, the first workmen's train being not yet due. And there they stood. Not another human being was abroad. Only the clock of St Bude's was faithfully awakening every soul within a radius of two hundred yards each quarter of an hour. Then a porter came and opened the gate – it was still exceedingly early – and Priam booked for Waterloo in triumph.

'Oh,' cried Alice, as they mounted the stairs, 'I quite forgot to draw up the blinds at the front of the house.' And she stopped on the stairs.

'What did you want to draw up the blinds for?'

'If they're down everybody will know instantly that we're gone. Whereas if I—'

She began to descend the stairs.

'Alice!' he said sharply, in a strange voice. The muscles of his white face were drawn.

'What!'

'D—n the blinds. Come along, or upon my soul I'll kill you!'

She realized that his nerves were in active insurrection, and that a mere nothing might bring about the fall of the government.

'Oh, very well!' She soothed him by her amiable obedience.

In a quarter of an hour they were safely lost in the wilderness of Waterloo and the newspaper train bore them off to Bournemouth for a few days' respite.

THE NATION'S CURIOSITY

The interest of the United Kingdom in the unique case of Witt *v.* Parfitts had already reached apparently the highest possible degree of intensity. And there was reason for the kingdom's passionate curiosity. Whitney Witt, the plaintiff, had come over to England, with his eccentricities, his retinue, his extreme wealth and his failing eyesight, specially to fight Parfitts. A half-pathetic figure, this white-haired man, once a connoisseur, who, from mere habit, continued to buy expensive pictures when he could no longer see them! Whitney Witt was implacably set against Parfitts, because he was convinced that Mr Oxford had sought to take advantage of his blindness. There he was, conducting his action regardless of expense. His apartments and his regal daily existence at the Grand Babylon alone cost a fabulous sum, which may be precisely ascertained by references to illustrated articles in the papers. Then Mr Oxford, the youngish Jew who had acquired Parfitts, who was Parfitts, also cut a picturesque figure on the face of London. He, too, was spending money with both hands; for Parfitts itself was at stake. Last, and most disturbing, was the individual looming mysteriously in the background, the inexplicable man who lived in Werter Road, and whose identity would be decided by the judgment in the case of Witt *v.* Parfitts. If Witt won his action, then Parfitts might retire from business. Mr Oxford would probably go to prison for having sold goods on false pretences, and the name of Henry Leek, valet, would be added to the list of adventurous scoundrels who have pretended to be their masters. But if Witt should lose – then what a complication, and what further enigmas to be solved! If Witt should lose, the national funeral of Priam Farll had been a fraudulent farce. A common valet lay under the hallowed stones of the Abbey, and Europe had mourned in vain! If Witt should lose, a gigantic and unprecedented swindle had been practised upon the nation. Then the question would arise, Why?

Hence it was not surprising that popular interest, nourished by an indefatigable and an excessively enterprising Press, should have mounted till no one would have believed that it could mount any more. But the evasion from Werter Road on that June morning intensified the interest enormously. Of course, owing to the drawn blinds, it soon became known, and the blood-hounds of the Sunday papers were sniffing along the platforms of all the termini in London. Priam's departure greatly prejudiced the cause of Mr Oxford, especially when the bloodhounds failed and Priam persisted in his invisibility. If a man was an honest man, why should he flee the public gaze, and in the night? There was but a step from the posing of this question to the inevitable inference that Mr Oxford's line of defence was really too fantastic for credence. Certainly organs of vast circulation, while repeating that, as the action was *sub judice*, they could say nothing about it, had already tried the action several times in their impartial columns, and they now tried it again, with the entire public as jury. And in three days Priam had definitely become a criminal in the public eye, a criminal flying from justice. Useless to assert that he was simply a witness subpoenaed to give evidence at the trial! He had transgressed the unwritten law of the English constitution that a person prominent in a *cause célèbre* belongs for the time being, not to himself, but to the nation at large. He had no claim to privacy. In surreptitiously obtaining seclusion he was merely robbing the public and the public's Press of their inalienable right.

Who could deny now the reiterated statement that he was a bigamist?

It came to be said that he must be on his way to South America. Then the public read avidly articles by specially retained barristers on the extradition treaties with Brazil, Argentina, Ecuador, Chili, Paraguay, and Uruguay.

The curates Matthew and Henry preached to crowded congregations at Putney and Bermondsey, and were reported verbatim in the 'Christian Voice Sermon Supplement,' and other messengers of light.

And gradually the nose of England bent closer and closer to its newspaper of a morning. And coffee went cold, and bacon fat

congealed, from the Isle of Wight to Hexham, while the latest
rumours were being swallowed. It promised to be stupendous,
dous, did the case of Witt *v*. Parfitts. It promised to be one of
those cases that alone makes life worth living, that alone
compensate for the horrors of climate, in England. And then
the day of hearing arrived, and the afternoon papers which
appear at nine o'clock in the morning announced that Henry
Leek (or Priam Farll, according to your wish) and his wife (or
his female companion and willing victim) had returned to
Werter Road. And England held its breath; and even Scotland
paused, expectant; and Ireland stirred in its Celtic dream.

MENTION OF TWO MOLES

The theatre in which the emotional drama of Witt *v*. Parfitts
was to be played lacked the usual characteristics of a modern
place of entertainment. It was far too high for its width and
breadth; it was badly illuminated; it was draughty in winter
and stuffy in summer, being completely deprived of ventilation.
lation. Had it been under the control of the County Council it
would have been instantly condemned as dangerous in case of
fire, for its gangways were always encumbered and its exits of
a mediaeval complexity. It had no stage, no footlights, and all
its seats were of naked wood except one.

This unique seat was occupied by the principal player, who
wore a humorous wig and a brilliant and expensive scarlet
costume. He was a fairly able judge, but he had mistaken his
vocation; his rare talent for making third-rate jokes would
have brought him a fortune in the world of musical comedy.
His salary was a hundred a week; better comedians have
earned less. On the present occasion he was in the midst of a
double row of fashionable hats, and beneath the hats were the
faces of fourteen feminine relatives and acquaintances. These
hats performed the function of 'dressing' the house. The
principal player endeavoured to behave as though under the
illusion that he was alone in his glory, but he failed.

There were four other leading actors: Mr Pennington,
K.C., and Mr Vodrey, K.C., engaged by the plaintiff; and Mr
Cass, K.C., and Mr Crepitude, K.C., engaged by the defend-

ant. These artistes were the stars of their profession, nominally less glittering, but really far more glittering, than the player in scarlet. Their wigs were of inferior quality to his, and their costumes shabby, but they did not mind, for whereas he got a hundred a week, they each got a hundred a day. Three junior performers received ten guineas a day apiece: one of them held a watching brief for the Dean and Chapter of the Abbey, who, being members of a Christian fraternity, were pained and horrified by the defendant's implication that they had given interment to a valet, and who were determined to resist exhumation by all hazards. The supers in the drama, whose business it was to whisper to each other and to the players, consisted of solicitors, solicitors' clerks, and experts; their combined emoluments worked out at the rate of a hundred and fifty pounds a day. Twelve excellent men in the jury-box received between them about as much as would have kept a K.C. alive for five minutes. The total expenses of production thus amounted to something like six or seven hundred pounds a day. The preliminary expenses had run into several thousands. The enterprise could have been made remunerative by hiring for it Covent Garden Theatre and selling stalls as for Tetrazzini and Caruso, but in the absurd auditorium chosen, crammed though it was to the perilous doors, the loss was necessarily terrific. Fortunately the affair was subsidized; not merely by the State, but also by those two wealthy capitalists, Whitney C. Witt and Mr Oxford; and therefore the management were in a position to ignore paltry financial considerations and to practise art for art's sake.

In opening the case Mr Pennington, K.C., gave instant proof of his astounding histrionic powers. He began calmly, colloquially, treating the jury as friends of his boyhood, and the judge as a gifted uncle, and stated in simple language that Whitney C. Witt was claiming seventy-two thousand pounds from the defendant, money paid for worthless pictures palmed off upon the myopic and venerable plaintiff as masterpieces. He recounted the life and death of the great painter Priam Farll, and his solemn burial amid the tears of the whole world. He dwelt upon the genius of Priam Farll, and then upon the confiding nature of the plaintiff. Then he inquired who could blame the plaintiff for his confidence in the uprightness of a

firm with such a name as Parfitts. And then he explained by
what accident of a dating-stamp on a canvas it had been
discovered that the pictures guaranteed to be by Priam Farll
were painted after Priam Farll's death.

He proceeded with no variation of tone: 'The explanation is
simplicity itself. Priam Farll was not really dead. It was his
valet who died. Quite naturally, quite comprehensibly, the
great genius Priam Farll, wished to pass the remainder of his
career as a humble valet. He deceived everybody; the doctor,
his cousin, Mr Duncan Farll, the public authorities, the Dean
and Chapter of the Abbey, the nation – in fact, the entire
world. As Henry Leek he married, and as Henry Leek he
recommended the art of painting – in Putney; he carried on the
vocation several years without arousing the suspicions of a
single person; and then – by a curious coincidence immediately
after my client threatened an action against the defendant – he
displayed himself in his true identity as Priam Farll. Such is the
simple explanation,' said Pennington, K.C., and added,
'which you will hear presently from the defendant. Doubtless
it will commend itself to you as experienced men of the world.
You cannot but have perceived that such things are constantly
happening in real life, that they are of daily occurrence. I am
almost ashamed to stand up before you and endeavour to rebut
a story so plausible and so essentially convincing. I feel that my
task is well-nigh hopeless. Nevertheless, I must do my best.'

And so on.

It was one of his greatest feats in the kind of irony that
appeals to a jury. And the audience deemed that the case was
already virtually decided.

After Whitney C. Witt and his secretary had been called and
had filled the court with the echoing twang of New York (the
controlled fury of the aged Witt was highly effective), Mrs
Henry Leek was invited to the witness-box. She was supported
thither by her two curates, who, however, could not prevent
her from weeping at the stern voice of the usher. She related her
marriage.

'Is that your husband?' demanded Vodrey, K.C. (who had
now assumed the principal rôle, Pennington, K.C., being
engaged in another play in another theatre), pointing with one
of his well-conceived dramatic gestures to Priam Farll.

'It is,' sobbed Mrs Henry Leek.

The unhappy creature believed what she said, and the curates, though silent, made a deep impression on the jury. In cross-examination, when Crepitude, K.C., forced her to admit that on first meeting Priam in his house in Werter Road she had not been quite sure of his identity, she replied –

'It's all come over me since. Shouldn't a woman recognize the father of her own children?'

'She should,' interpolated the judge. There was a difference of opinion as to whether his word was jocular or not.

Mrs Henry Leek was a touching figure, but not amusing. It was Mr Duncan Farll who, quite unintentionally, supplied the first relief.

Duncan pooh-poohed the possibility of Priam being Priam. He detailed all the circumstances that followed the death in Selwood Terrace, and showed in fifty ways that Priam could not have been Priam. The man now masquerading as Priam was not even a gentleman, whereas Priam was Duncan's cousin! Duncan was an excellent witness, dry, precise, imperturbable. Under cross-examination by Crepitude he had to describe particularly his boyish meeting with Priam. Mr Crepitude was not inquisitive.

'Tell us what occurred,' said Crepitude.

'Well, we fought.'

'Oh! You fought! What did you two naughty boys fight about?' (Great laughter.)

'About a plum cake, I think.'

'Oh! Not a seed cake, a plum cake?' (Great laughter.)

'I think a plum cake.'

'And what was the result of this sanguinary encounter?' (Great laughter.)

'My cousin loosened one of my teeth.' (Great laughter, in which the court joined.)

'And what did you do to him?'

'I'm afraid I didn't do much. I remember tearing half his clothes off.' (Roars of laughter, in which every one joined except Priam and Duncan Farll.)

'Oh! You are sure you remember that? You are sure that it wasn't he who tore *your* clothes off?' (Lots of hysteric laughter.)

'Yes,' said Duncan, coldly dreaming in the past. His eyes had the 'far-away' look as he added, 'I remember now that my cousin had two little moles on his neck below the collar. I seem to remember seeing them. I've just thought of it.'

There is, of course, when it is mentioned in a theatre, something exorbitantly funny about even one mole. Two moles together brought the house down.

Mr Crepitude leaned over to a solicitor in front of him; the solicitor leaned aside to a solicitor's clerk, and the solicitor's clerk whispered to Priam Farll, who nodded.

'Er—' Mr Crepitude was beginning again, but he stopped and said to Duncan Farll, 'Thank you. You can step down.'

Then a witness named Justini, a cashier at the Hôtel de Paris, Monte Carlo, swore that Priam Farll, the renowned painter, had spent four days in the Hôtel de Paris one hot May, seven years ago, and that the person in the court whom the defendant stated to be Priam Farll was not that man. No cross-examination could shake Mr Justini. Following him came the manager of the Hôtel Belvedere at Mount Pélerin, near Vevey, Switzerland, who related a similar tale and was equally unshaken.

And after that the pictures themselves were brought in, and the experts came after them and technical evidence was begun. Scarcely had it begun when a clock struck, and the performance ended for the day. The principal actors doffed their costumes, and snatched up the evening papers to make sure that the descriptive reporters had been as eulogistic of them as usual. The judge, who subscribed to a Press-cutting agency, was glad to find, the next morning, that none of his jokes had been omitted by any of the nineteen chief London dailies. And the Strand and Piccadilly were quick with Witt *v.* Parfitts – on evening posters and in the strident mouths of newsboys. The telegraph wires vibrated to Witt *v.* Parfitts. In the great betting industrial towns of the provinces wagers were laid at scientific prices. England, in a word, was content, and the principal actors had the right to be content also. Very astute people in clubs and saloon bars talked darkly about those two moles, and Priam's nod in response to the whispers of the solicitor's clerk: such details do not escape the modern sketch writer at a thousand a year. To very astute people the two moles appeared to promise pretty things.

PRIAM'S REFUSAL

'Leek in the box.'

This legend got itself on to the telegraph wires and the placards within a few minutes of Priam's taking the oath. It sent a shiver of anticipation throughout the country. Three days had passed since the opening of the case (for actors engaged at a hundred a day for the run of the piece do not crack whips behind experts engaged at ten or twenty a day; the pace had therefore been dignified), and England wanted a fillip.

Nobody except Alice knew what to expect from Priam. Alice knew. She knew that Priam was in an extremely peculiar state which might lead to extremely peculiar results; and she knew also that there was nothing to be done with him! She herself had made one little effort to bathe him in the light of reason; the effort had not succeeded. She saw the danger of renewing it. Pennington, K.C., by the way, insisted that she should leave the court during Priam's evidence.

Priam's attitude towards the whole case was one of bitter resentment, a resentment now hot, now cold. He had the strongest possible objection to the entire affair. He hated Witt as keenly as he hated Oxford. All that he demanded from the world was peace and quietness, and the world would not grant him these inexpensive commodities. He had not asked to be buried in Westminster Abbey; his interment had been forced upon him. And if he chose to call himself by another name why should he not do so? If he chose to marry a simple woman, and live in a suburb and paint pictures at ten pounds each, why should he not do so? Why should he be dragged out of his tranquility because two persons in whom he felt no interest whatever, had quarrelled over his pictures! Why should his life have been made unbearable in Putney by the extravagant curiosity of a mob of journalists? And then, why should he be compelled, by means of a piece of blue paper, to go through the frightful ordeal and flame of publicity in a witness-box? That was the crowning unmerited torture, the unthinkable horror which had broken his sleep for many nights.

In the box he certainly had all the appearance of a trapped criminal, with his nervous movements, his restless lowered eyes, and his faint, hard voice that he could scarcely fetch up from his throat. Nervousness lined with resentment forms excellent material for the plastic art of a cross-examination counsel, and Pennington, K.C., itched to be at work; Crepitude, K.C., Oxford's counsel, was in less joyous mood. Priam was Crepitude's own witness, and yet a horrible witness, a witness who had consistently and ferociously declined to open his mouth until he was in the box. Assuredly he had nodded, in response to the whispered question of the solicitor's clerk, but he had not confirmed the nod, nor breathed a word of assistance during the three days of the trial. He had merely sat there blazing in silence.

'Your name is Priam Farll?' began Crepitude.

'It is,' said Priam sullenly, and with all the external characteristics of a liar. At intervals he glanced surreptitiously at the judge, as though the judge had been a bomb with a lighted fuse.

The examination started badly, and it went from worse to worse. The idea that this craven, prevaricating figure in the box could be the illustrious, the world-renowned Priam Farll seemed absurd. Crepitude had to exercise all his self-control in order not to bully Priam.

'That is all,' said Crepitude, after Priam had given his preposterous and halting explanations of the strange phenomena of his life after the death of Leek. None of these carried conviction. He merely said that the woman Leek was mistaken in identifying him as her husband; he inferred that she was hysterical. This inference alienated him from the audience completely. His statement that he had no definite reason for pretending to be Leek – that it was an impulse of the moment – was received with mute derision. His explanation, when questioned as to the evidence of the hotel officials, that more than once his valet Leek had gone about impersonating his master, seemed grotesquely inadequate.

People wondered why Crepitude had made no reference to the moles. The fact was, Crepitude was afraid to refer to the moles. In mentioning the moles to Priam he might be staking all to lose all.

However, Pennington, K.C., alluded to the moles. But not until he had conclusively proved to the judge in a cross-examination of two hours' duration, that Priam knew nothing of Priam's own youth, nor of painting, nor of the world of painters. He made a sad mess of Priam. And Priam's voice grew fainter and fainter, and his gestures more and more self-incriminating.

Pennington, K.C., achieved one or two brilliant little effects.

'Now, you say you went with the defendant to his club, and that he told you of the difficulty he was in!'

'Yes.'

'Did he make you any offer of money?'

'Yes.'

'Ah! What did he offer you?'

'Thirty-six thousand pounds.' (Sensation in court.)

'So! And what was this thirty-six thousand pounds to be for?'

'I don't know.'

'You don't know? Come now.'

'I don't know.'

'You accepted the offer?'

'No, I refused it.' (Sensation in court.)

'Why did you refuse it?'

'Because I didn't care to accept it.'

'Then no money passed between you that day?'

'Yes. Five hundred pounds.'

'What for?'

'A picture.'

'The same kind of picture that you had been selling for ten pounds?'

'Yes.'

'So that on the very day that the defendant wanted you to swear that you were Priam Farll, the price of your pictures rose from ten pounds to five hundred?'

'Yes.'

'Doesn't that strike you as odd?'

'Yes.'

'You still say – mind, Leek, you are on your oath! – you still say that you refused thirty-six thousand pounds in order to accept five hundred?'

'I sold a picture for five hundred.'

(On the placards in the Strand: 'Severe cross-examination of Leek.')

'Now about the encounter with Mr Duncan Farll. Of course, if you are really Priam Farll, you remember all about that?'

'Yes.'

'What age were you?'

'I don't know. About nine.'

'Oh! You were about nine. A suitable age for cake.' (Great laughter.) 'Now, Mr Duncan Farll says you loosened one of his teeth.'

'I did.'

'And that he tore your clothes.'

'I dare say.'

'He says he remembers the fact because you had two moles.'

'Yes.'

'Have you two moles?'

'Yes.' (Immense sensation.)

Pennington paused.

'Where are they?'

'On my neck just below my collar.'

'Kindly place your hand at the spot.'

Priam did so. The excitement was terrific.

Pennington again paused. But, convinced that Priam was an impostor, he sarcastically proceeded –

'Perhaps, if I am not asking too much, you will take your collar off and show the two moles to the court?'

'No,' said Priam stoutly. And for the first time he looked Pennington in the face.

'You would prefer to do it, perhaps, in his lordship's room, if his lordship consents.'

'I won't do it anywhere, my lord,' Priam repeated loudly. All his resentment surged up once more; and particularly his resentment against the little army of experts who had pronounced his pictures to be clever but worthless imitations of himself. If his pictures, admittedly painted after his supposed death, could not prove his identity; if his word was to be flouted by insulting and bewigged beasts of prey; then his moles should not prove his identity. He resolved upon obstinacy.

'The witness, gentlemen,' said Pennington, K.C., in triumph to the jury, 'has two moles on his neck exactly as described by Mr Duncan Farll, but he will not display them!'

Eleven legal minds bent nobly to the problem whether the law and justice of England could compel a free man to take his collar off if he refused to take his collar off. In the meantime, of course, the case had to proceed. The six or seven hundred pounds a day must be earned, and there were various other witnesses. The next witness was Alice.

CHAPTER XII

ALICE'S PERFORMANCES

When Alice was called, and when she stood up in the box, and, smiling indulgently at the doddering usher, kissed the book as if it had been a chubby nephew, a change came over the emotional atmosphere of the court, which felt a natural need to smile. Alice was in all her best clothes, but it cannot be said that she looked the wife of a super-eminent painter. In answer to a question she stated that before marrying Priam she was the widow of a builder in a small way of business, well known in Putney and also in Wandsworth. This was obviously true. She could have been nothing but the widow of a builder in a small way of business well known in Putney and also in Wandsworth. She was every inch that.

'How did you first meet your present husband, Mrs Leek?' asked Mr Crepitude.

'Mrs Farll, if you please,' she cheerfully corrected him.

'Well, Mrs Farll, then.'

'I must say,' she remarked conversationally, 'it seems queer you should be calling me Mrs Leek, when they're paying you to prove that I'm Mrs Farll, Mr —. Excuse me, I forget your name.'

This nettled Crepitude, K.C., It nettled him, too, merely to see a witness standing in the box just as if she were standing in her kitchen talking to a tradesman at the door. He was not accustomed to such a spectacle. And though Alice was his own witness he was angry with her because he was angry with her husband. He blushed. Juniors behind him could watch the blush creeping like a tide round the back of his neck over his exceedingly white collar.

'If you'll be good enough to reply—' said he.

'I met my husband outside St George's Hall, by appointment,' said she.

'But before that. How did you make his acquaintance?'

'Through a matrimonial agency,' said she.

'Oh!' observed Crepitude, and decided that he would not pursue that avenue. The fact was Alice had put him into the wrong humour for making the best of her. She was, more-over, in a very difficult position, for Priam had positively forbidden her to have any speech with solicitor's clerks or with solicitors, and thus Crepitude knew not what pitfalls for him her evidence might contain. He drew from her an expression of opinion that her husband was the real Priam Farll, but she could give no reasons in support – did not seem to conceive that reasons in support were necessary.

'Has your husband any moles?' asked Crepitude suddenly.

'Any what?' demanded Alice, leaning forward.

Vodrey, K.C., sprang up.

'I submit to your lordship that my learned friend is putting a leading question,' said Vodrey, K.C.

'Mr Crepitude,' said the judge, 'can you not phrase your questions differently?'

'Has your husband any birthmarks – er – on his body?' Crepitude tried again.

'Oh! *Moles*, you said? You needn't be afraid. Yes, he's got two moles, close together on his neck, here.' And she pointed amid silence to the exact spot. Then, noticing the silence, she added, 'That's all that I *know* of.'

Crepitude resolved to end his examinations upon this impressive note, and he sat down. And Alice had Vodrey, K.C., to face.

'You met your husband through a matrimonial agency?' he asked.

'Yes.'

'Who first had recourse to the agency?'

'I did.'

'And what was your object?'

'I wanted to find a husband, of course,' she smiled. 'What *do* people go to matrimonial agencies for?'

'You aren't here to put questions to me,' said Vodrey severely.

'Well,' she said, 'I should have thought you would have known what people went to matrimonial agencies for. Still, you live and learn.' She sighed cheerfully.

'Do you think a matrimonial agency is quite the nicest way of—'

'It depends what you mean by "nice,"' said Alice.

'Womanly.'

'Yes.' said Alice shortly, 'I do. If you're going to stand there and tell me I am unwomanly, all I have to say is that you're unmanly.'

'You say you first met your husband outside St George's Hall?'

'Yes.'

'Never seen him before?'

'No.'

'How did you recognize him?'

'By his photograph?'

'Oh, he'd sent you his photograph?'

'Yes.'

'With a letter?'

'Yes.'

'In what name was the letter signed?'

'Henry Leek.'

'Was that before or after the death of the man who was buried in Westminster Abbey?'

'A day or two before.' (Sensation in court.)

'So that your present husband was calling himelf Henry Leek before the death?'

'No, he wasn't. That letter was written by the man that died.
My husband found my reply to it, and my photograph, in the
man's bag afterwards; and happening to be strolling past St
George's Hall just at the moment like—'

'Well, happening to be strolling past St George's Hall just at
that moment like—' (Titters.)

'I caught sight of him and spoke to him. You see, I thought
then that he was the man who wrote the letter.'

'What made you think so?'

'I had the photograph.'

'So that the man who wrote the letter and died didn't send his
own photograph. He sent another photograph – the photograph
of your husband?'

'Yes, didn't you know that? I should have thought you'd have
known that.'

'Do you really expect the jury to believe that tale?'

Alice turned smiling to the jury. 'No,' she said. 'I'm not sure
as I do. I didn't believe it myself for a long time. But it's true.'

'Then at first you didn't believe your husband was the real
Priam Farll?'

'No. You see, he didn't exactly tell me like. He only sort of
hinted.'

'But you didn't believe?'

'No.'

'You thought he was lying?'

'No, I thought it was just a kind of an idea he had. You know
my husband isn't like other gentlemen.'

'I imagine not,' said Vodrey. 'Now, when did you come to be
perfectly sure that your husband was the real Priam Farll?'

'It was the night of that day when Mr Oxford came down to
see him. He told me all about it then.'

'Oh! That day when Mr Oxford paid him five hundred
pounds?'

'Yes.'

'Immediately Mr Oxford paid him five hundred pounds you
were ready to believe that your husband was the real Priam Farll.
Doesn't that strike you as excessively curious?'.

'It's just how it happened,' said Alice blandly.

'Now about these moles. You pointed to the right side of your
neck. Are you sure they aren't on the left side?'

'Let me think now,' said Alice, frowning. 'When he's shaving in a morning – he gets up earlier now than he used to – I can see his face in the looking-glass, and in the looking-glass the moles are on the left side. So on *him* they must be on the right side. Yes, the right side. That's it.'

'Have you never seen them except in a mirror, my good woman?' interpolated the judge.

For some reason Alice flushed. 'I suppose you think that's funny,' she answered, slightly tossing her head.

The audience expected the roof to fall. But the roof withstood the strain, thanks to a sagacious deafness on the part of the judge. If, indeed, he had not been visited by a sudden deafness, it is difficult to see how he would have handled the situation.

'Have you any idea,' Vodrey inquired, 'why your husband refuses to submit his neck to the inspection of the court?'

'I didn't know he had refused.'

'But he has.'

'Well,' said Alice, 'if you hadn't turned me out of the court while he was being examined, perhaps I could have told you. But I can't as it is. So it serves you right.'

Thus ended Alice's performance.

THE PUBLIC CAPTIOUS

The court rose, and another six or seven hundred pounds was gone into the pockets of the celebrated artistes engaged. It became at once obvious, from the tone of the evening placards and the contents of evening papers, and the remarks in crowded suburban trains, that for the public the trial had resolved itself into an affair of moles. Nothing else now interested the great and intelligent public. If Priam had those moles on his neck, then he was the real Priam. If he had not, then he was a common cheat. The public had taken the matter into its own hands. The sturdy common sense of the public was being applied to the affair. On the whole it may be said that the sturdy common sense of the public was against Priam. For the majority, the entire story was fishily preposterous. It must surely be clear to the feeblest brain that if Priam possessed moles he would expose them. The minority, who talked of psychology and the artistic tempera-

ment, were regarded as the cousins of Little Englanders and the
direct descendants of pro-Boers.

Still, the thing ought to be proved or disproved.

Why didn't the judge commit him for contempt of court? He
would then be sent to Holloway and be compelled to strip – and
there you were!'

Or why didn't Oxford hire some one to pick a quarrel with
him in the street and carry the quarrel to blows, with a view to
raiment tearing?

A nice thing, English justice – if it had no machinery to force a
man to show his neck to a jury! But then English justice *was*
notoriously comic.

And whole trainfuls of people sneered at their country's
institution in a manner which, had it been adopted by a
foreigner, would have plunged Europe into war and finally
tested the bluewater theory. Undoubtedly the immemorial
traditions of English justice came in for very severe handling
simply because Priam would not take his collar off.

And he would not.

The next morning there were consultations in counsel's
rooms, and the common law of the realm was ransacked to find
a legal method of inspecting Priam's moles, without success.
Priam arrived safely at the courts with his usual high collar, and
was photographed thirty times between the kerb and the
entrance hall.

'He's slept in it!' cried wags.

'Bet yer two ter one it's a clean 'un!' cried other wags. 'His
missus gets his linen up.'

It was subject to such indignities that the man who had defied
the Supreme Court of Judicature reached his seat in the theatre.
When solicitors and counsel attempted to reason with him, he
answered with silence. The rumour ran that in his hip pocket he
was carryng a revolver wherewith to protect the modesty of his
neck.

The celebrated artistes, having perceived the folly of losing six
or seven hundred pounds a day because Priam happened to be an
obstinate idiot, continued with the case. For Mr Oxford and
another army of experts of European reputation were waiting to
prove that the pictures admittedly painted after the burial in the
National Valhalla were painted by Priam Farll, and could have

been painted by no other. They demonstrated this by internal evidence. It was a phenomenon eminently legal. And Priam, in his stiff collar, sat and listened.

The experts, however, achieved two feats, both unintentionally. They sent the judge soundly to sleep, and they wearied the public, which considered that the trial was falling short of its early promise. This *expertise* went on to the extent of two whole days and appreciably more than another thousand pounds. And on the third day Priam, somewhat hardened to renown, reappeared with his mysterious neck, and more determined than ever. He had seen in a paper, which was otherwise chiefly occupied with moles and experts, a cautious statement that the police had collected the necessary prima facie evidence of bigamy, and that his arrest was imminent. However, something stranger than arrest for bigamy happened to him.

NEW EVIDENCE

The principal King's Bench corridor in the Law Courts, like the other main corridors, is a place of strange meetings and interviews. A man may receive there a bit of news that will change the whole of the rest of his life, or he may receive only an invitation to a mediocre lunch in the restaurant underneath; he never knows beforehand. Priam assuredly did not receive an invitation to lunch. He was traversing the crowded thoroughfares – for with the exception of match and toothpick sellers the corridor has the characteristics of a Strand pavement in the forenoon – when he caught sight of Mr Oxford talking to a woman. Now, he had exchanged no word with Mr Oxford since the historic scene in the club, and he was determined to exchange no word; however, they had not gone through the formality of an open breach. The most prudent thing to do, therefore, was to turn and take another corridor. And Priam would have fled, being capable of astonishing prudence when prudence meant the avoidance of unpleasant encounters; but, just as he was turning, the woman in conversation with Mr Oxford saw him, and stepped towards him with the rapidity of thought, holding forth her hand. She was tall, thin, and stiffly distinguished in the brusque, Dutch-doll motions of her limbs.

Her coat and skirt were quite presentable, but her feet were large (not her fault, of course, though one is apt to treat large feet as a crime), and her feathered hat was even larger. She hid her age behind a veil.

'How do you do, Mr Farll?' she addressed him firmly, in a voice which nevertheless throbbed.

It was Lady Sophia Entwistle.

'How do you do?' he said, taking her offered hand.

There was nothing else to do, and nothing else to say.

Then Mr Oxford put out his hand.

'How do you do, Mr Farll?'

And, taking Mr Oxford's hated hand, Priam said again, 'How do you do?'

It was all just as if there had been no past; the past seemed to have been swallowed up in the ordinariness of the crowded corridor. By all the rules for the guidance of human conduct, Lady Sophia ought to have denounced Priam with outstretched dramatic finger to the contempt of the world as a philanderer with the hearts of trusting women; and he ought to have kicked Mr Oxford along the corridor for a scheming Hebrew. But they merely shook hands and asked each other how they did, not even expecting an answer. This shows to what extent the ancient qualities of the race have deteriorated.

Then a silence.

'I suppose you know, Mr Farll,' said Lady Sophia, rather suddenly, 'that I have got to give evidence in this case?'

'No,' he said, 'I didn't.'

'Yes, it seems they have scoured all over the Continent in vain to find people who knew you under your proper name, and who could identify you with certainty, and they couldn't find one – doubtless owing to your peculiar habits of travel.'

'Really,' said Priam.

He had made love to this woman. He had kissed her. They had promised to marry each other. It was a piece of wild folly on his part; but, in the eyes of an impartial person, folly could not excuse his desertion of her, his flight from her intellectual charms. His gaze pierced her veil. No, she was not quite so old as Alice. She was not more plain than Alice. She certainly knew more than Alice. She could talk about pictures without sticking a knife into his soul and turning it in the wound. She was better dressed than Alice. And her behaviour on the present occasion, candid, kind, correct, could not have been surpassed by Alice. And yet . . . Her demeanour was without question prodigiously splendid in its ignoring of all that she had gone through. And yet . . . Even in that moment of complicated misery he had enough strength to hate her because he had been fool enough to make love to her. No excuse whatever for him, of course!

'I was in India when I first heard of this case,' Lady Sophia continued. 'At first I thought it must be a sort of Tichborne business over again. Then, knowing you as I did, I thought perhaps it wasn't.'

'And as Lady Sophia happens to be in London now,' put in Mr Oxford, 'she is good enough to give her invaluable evidence on my behalf.'

'That is scarcely the way to describe it,' said Lady Sophia coldly. 'I am only here because you compel me to be here by subpoena. It is all due to your acquaintanceship with my aunt.'

'Quite so, quite so!' Mr Oxford agreed. 'It naturally can't be very agreeable to you to have to go into the witness-box and submit to cross-examination. Certainly not. And I am the more obliged to you for your kindness, Lady Sophia.'

Priam comprehended the situation. Lady Sophia, after his supposed death, had imparted to relatives the fact of his engagement, and the unscrupulous scoundrel, Mr Oxford, had got hold of her and was forcing her to give evidence for him. And after the evidence, the joke of every man in the street would be to the effect that Priam Farll, rather than marry the skinny spinster, had pretended to be dead.

'You see,' Mr Oxford added to him, 'the important point about Lady Sophia's evidence is that in Paris she saw both you and your valet – the valet obviously a servant, and you obviously his master. There can, therefore, be no question of her having been deceived by the valet posing as the master. It is a most fortunate thing that by a mere accident I got on the tracks of Lady Sophia in time. In the nick of time. Only yesterday afternoon!'

No reference by Mr Oxford to Priam's obstinacy in the matter of collars. He appeared to regard Priam's collar as a phenomenon of Nature, such as the weather, or a rock in the sea, as something to be accepted with resignation! No sign of annoyance with Priam! He was the prince of diplomatists, was Mr Oxford.

'Can I speak to you a minute?' said Lady Sophia to Priam.

Mr Oxford stepped away with a bow.

And Lady Sophia looked steadily at Priam. He had to admit again that she was stupendous. She was his capital mistake; but she was stupendous.

At their last interview he had embraced her. She had attended his funeral in Westminster Abbey. And she could suppress all that from her eyes! She could stand there calm and urbane in her acceptance of the terrific past. Apparently she forgave.

Said Lady Sophia simply, 'Now, Mr Farll, shall I have to give evidence or not? You know it depends on you?'

The casualness of her tone was sublime; it was heroic; it made her feet small.

He had sworn to himself that he would be cut in pieces before he would aid the unscrupulous Mr Oxford by removing his collar in presence of those dramatic artistes. He had been grossly insulted, disturbed, maltreated, and exploited. The entire world had meddled with his private business, and he would be cut in pieces before he would display those moles which would decide the issue in an instant.

Well, she had cut him in pieces.

'Please don't worry,' said he in reply. 'I will attend to things.'

At that moment Alice, who had followed him by a later train, appeared.

'Good morning, Lady Sophia,' he said, raising his hat, and left her.

THOUGHTS ON JUSTICE

'Farll takes his collar off.' 'Witt v. Parfitts. Result.' These and similar placards flew in the Strand breezes. Never in the history of empires had the removal of a starched linen collar (size 16½) created one-thousandth part of the sensation caused by the removal of this collar. It was an epoch-making act. It finished the drama of Witt v. Parfitts. The renowned artistes engaged did not, of course, permit the case to collapse at once. No it had to be concluded slowly and majestically, with due forms and expenses. New witnesses (such as doctors) had to be called, and old ones recalled. Duncan Farll, for instance, had to be recalled, and if the situation was ignominious for Priam it was also ignominious for Duncan. Duncan's sole advantage in his defeat was that the judge did not skin him alive in the summing up, nor the jury in their verdict. England breathed more freely when the affair was fully over and the renowned artistes engaged had withdrawn enveloped in glory. The truth was that England, so proud of her systems, had had a fright. Her judicial methods had very nearly failed to make a man take his collar off in public. They had really failed, but it had all come right in the end, and so England pretended that they had only just missed failing. A grave injustice would have been perpetuated had Priam chosen not to take off his collar. People said, naturally, that imprisonment for bigamy would have included the taking off of collars; but then it was rumoured that prosecution for bigamy had not by any means been a certainty, as since leaving the box Mrs Henry Leek had wavered in her identification. However, the justice of England had emerged safely. And it was all very astounding and shocking and improper. And everybody was exceedingly wise after the event. And with one voice the Press cried that something painful ought to occur at once to Priam Farll, no matter how great an artist he was.

The question was: How could Priam be trapped in the net of the law? He had not committed bigamy. He had done nothing. He had only behaved in a negative manner. He had not even given false information to the registrar. And Dr Cashmore could throw no light on the episode, for he was dead. His wife and daughters had at last succeeded in killing him. The judge had intimated that the ecclesiastical wrath of the Dean and Chapter might speedily and terribly overtake Priam Farll; but that sounded vague and unsatisfactory to the lay ear.

In short, the matter was the most curious that ever was. And for the sake of the national peace of mind, the national dignity, and the national conceit, it was allowed to drop into forgetfulness after a few days. And when the papers announced that, by Priam's wish, the Farll museum was to be carried to completion and formally conveyed to the nation, despite all, the nation decided to accept that honourable amend, and went off to the seaside for its annual holiday.

THE WILL TO LIVE

Alice insisted on it, and so, immediately before their final departure from England, they went. Priam pretended that the visit was undertaken solely to please her; but the fact is that his own morbid curiosity moved in the same direction. They travelled by an omnibus past the Putney Empire and the Walham Green Empire as far as Walham Green, and there changed into another one which carried them past the Chelsea Empire, the Army and Navy Stores, and the Hotel Windsor to the doors of Westminster Abbey. And they vanished out of the October sunshine into the beamshot gloom of Valhalla. It was Alice's first view of Valhalla, though of course she had heard of it. In old times she had not had leisure to get round as far as Valhalla. It impressed her deeply. A verger pointed them to the nave; but they dared not demand more minute instructions. They had not the courage to ask for *It*. Priam could not speak. There were moments with him when he could not speak lest his soul should come out of his mouth and flit irrecoverably away. And he could not find the tomb. Save for the outrageous tomb of mighty Newton, the nave seemed to be as naked as when it came into the world. Yet he was sure he was buried in the nave – and only three years ago, too! Astounding, was it not, what could happen in three years?

He knew that the tomb had not been removed, for there had been an article in the 'Daily Record' on the previous day asking in the name of a scandalized public whether the Dean and Chapter did not consider that three months was more than long enough for the correction of a fundamental error in the burial department. He was gloomy; he had in truth been somewhat gloomy ever since the trial. Perhaps it was the shadow of the wrath of the Dean and Chapter on him. He had ceased to procure joy in the daily manifestations of life in the streets of the town. And this failure to discover the tomb intensified the calm, amiable sadness which distinguished him.

Alice, gazing around, chiefly with her mouth, inquired suddenly –

'What's the printing there?'

She had detected a legend incised on one of the small stone flags which form the vast floor of the nave. They stooped over it.

'PRIAM FARLL,' it said simply, in fine Roman letters, and then the dates. That was all. Near by, on other flags, they deciphered other names of honour. This austere method of marking the repose of the dead commended itself to him, caused him to feel proud of himself and of the ridiculous England that somehow keeps our great love. His gloom faded. And do you know what idea rushed from his heart to his brain? 'By Jove!' I will paint finer pictures than any I've done yet!' And the impulse to recommence the work of creation surged over him. The tears started to his eyes.

'I like that!' murmured Alice, gazing at the stone, 'I do think that's nice.'

And *he* said, because he truly felt it, because the will to live raged through him again, tingling and smarting –

'I'm glad I'm not there.'

They smiled at each other, and their instinctive hands fumblingly met.

ON BOARD

A few days later, the Dean and Chapter, stung into action by the majestic rebuke of the 'Daily Record,' amended the floor of Valhalla and caused the mortal residuum of the immortal organism known as Henry Leek to be nocturnally transported to a different bed.

A few days later, also, a North German Lloyd steamer quitted Southampton for Algiers, bearing among its passengers Priam and Alice. It was a rough starlit night, and from the stern of the vessel the tumbled white water made a pathway straight to receding England. Priam had come to love the slopes of Putney with the broad river at the foot; but he showed what I think was a nice feeling in leaving England. His sojourn in our land had not crowned him with brilliance. He was not a being created for society, nor for cutting a figure, nor for exhibiting tact and prudence in the crises of existence. He could neither talk well nor read well, nor express himself in exactly suitable actions. He could only express himself at the end of a brush. He could only paint extremely beautiful pictures. That was the major part of his vitality. In minor ways he may have been, upon occasions, a

fool. But he was never a fool on canvas. He said everything
there, and said it to perfection, for those who could read, for
those who can read, and for those who will be able to read five
hundred years hence. Why expect more from him? Why be
disappointed in him? One does not expect a wire-walker to play
fine billiards. You yourself, mirror of prudence that you are,
would have certainly avoided all Priam's manifold errors in the
conduct of his social career; but you see, he was divine in another
way.

As the steamer sped along the lengthening pathway from
England, one question kept hopping in and out of his mind –

'*I wonder what they'll do with me next time?*'

Do not imagine that he and Alice were staring over the stern at
the singular isle. No! There were imperative reasons, which
affected both of them, against that. It was only in the moments
of the comparative calm which always follows insurrections that
Priam had leisure to wonder, and to see his limitations, and
joyfully to meditate upon the prospect of age devoted to the sole
doing of that which he could do so supremely, in a sweet exile
with the enchantress Alice.

ARNOLD BENNETT

THE MATADOR OF THE FIVE TOWNS

When Mr Loring, a visitor from London, is forced upon the hospitality of Dr Stirling, he becomes caught up in a sequence of totally unexpected events, and ends up experiencing the frenzied atmosphere of a football match in which Jos Myatt, 'The Matador of the Five Towns', is playing. But when the finest full-back in the league arrives at the doctor's house, events become more sombre . . .

Will Arthur Cotterill make it to London in time for his appointment? He doesn't think so when he wakes up, believing he has twenty minutes to get to the station. Fortunately his brother, Simeon, had put the clock on and disaster is averted. But this is only the first of many occasions on which Arthur's heart is set racing. 'Catching the Train' is Arnold Bennett at his most entertaining.

Both tragic and humorous, the stories in *The Matador of the Five Towns* chronicle events in the everyday lives of the Potteries' citizens.

ARNOLD BENNETT

TALES OF THE FIVE TOWNS

After a drink with Mr Gordon, 'a municipal mediocrity', Mr Curtenty, the Deputy-Mayor, makes the decision to purchase a flock of geese and drive them back to his residence. The problems he encounters soon become common knowledge and when the *Signal* reveals that the Mayor has resigned, it appears that 'His Worship the Goosedriver' will become a laughing-stock.

In 'The Hungarian Rhapsody' Edward Norris, under the impression that he is about to die, reveals to his wife that he has not been honest in a deal with her deceased father. Although she forgives him, the atmosphere remains tense, until May Norris says that she has something to tell her husband . . .

'His Worship the Goosedriver' and 'The Hungarian Rhapsody' are two of the stories in *Tales of the Five Towns*, in which Bennett tells of life in the Potteries and its citizens' adventures in London.

WILKIE COLLINS

THE YELLOW MASK & OTHER STORIES

The letter was anonymous but its message unmistakable: 'Neglect my advice and you will repent it to the end of your life. I have reasons for what I say – serious, fatal reasons, which I cannot divulge. If you would let your wife lie easy in her grave, if you would avoid a terrible warning, go not to the masked ball!'

The ball at the Melani Palace promised to be sensational, the old Marquis had a reputation as the most hospitable, as well as the most eccentric man in Pisa. Arcadian bowers, fantastic dances, the extravagant disguises were but a few of the attractions, until the Yellow Mask appeared – silent, inscrutable, relentless, gliding from room to room . . .

Told as the curious anecdotes of a poor painter, 'The Yellow Mask', together with 'Sister Rose' and 'A Stolen Letter', make up another superb collection from this master storyteller.

WILKIE COLLINS

HEART AND SCIENCE

Following the death of her father, Carmina finds herself placed under the guardianship of her aunt. Forced to leave her childhood home to live, friendless, in a strange country, her only consolation is the love of her cousin, Ovid Vere. When he is forced to leave Carmina to go abroad for the sake of his health, she is left at the mercy of her heartless aunt who has control over her substantial inheritance until her marriage. Still distressed by her bereavement, and left by Ovid to her aunt's devices, Carmina succumbs to illness, which is treated by the sinister and paranoid Dr Benjulia. But has he Carmina's best interests at heart in prescribing her treatment, or does his obsession with research into brain diseases lead his decisions?

In this book Wilkie Collins displays his mastery of suspense, increasing the tension step by step as he traces the human failings which persecute a friendless girl.